DISCLAIMER

Both this story and the characters within are fictitious. Therefore, any similarities to people or events are purely coincidental.

1

TESS

Hungry. Scared. Alone. Same feelings, different day, but once again, I had very few choices.

This had been my life on repeat for many more years than I care to remember, though I knew I'd brought this particular situation on myself. After all, it was my idea to run away to London, yet it didn't feel like I had a safer option at the time.

I thought back to that last day at the children's home where I'd lived for eighteen months. Nearly a week had gone by since I made my escape from The Willows, right under the noses of three residential social workers and two police officers.

Digging deep in my pockets, I found the last few pounds I had left. Even the emergency stash in my backpack had been long since spent. The money I now held in my hand came from begging at the side of a homeless guy whom I befriended my first night of sleeping rough.

I'd sneaked onto the train at Doncaster, staying hidden from the conductor until we reached King's Cross. It was getting late by the time I walked into central London, and the chaos of rush hour was almost at an end. I'd looked around for a hostel to stay in but couldn't get a place that night, so I carried on walking, stopping at a McDonald's for a burger and a hot drink to keep warm.

There were so many homeless people sleeping rough. Most of them looked scary and dirty, maybe even high. You shouldn't judge a person when you don't know their circumstances—I know that more than most, but being homeless was new to me, even if being scared wasn't, so you can forgive me for being frightened, and a little judgemental.

By the time I came across Danny, I was mentally and physically exhausted, and I'd stumbled over his legs as he slid them into his sleeping bag. He'd immediately jumped up to help me, apologising profusely, and from out of nowhere, I felt a wet lick on my ear as his little dog, Bess, fussed over me.

Danny had been sleeping rough for over four weeks since being evicted from his flat. He was an ex-soldier who'd come back from Afghanistan with PTSD, along with injuries sustained from a roadside IED that left him with a permanent limp.

He told me how lucky he was to survive the blast because three of his colleagues hadn't. They'd given him a flat and financial help, along with counselling. But Danny failed to go to some of the sessions when anxiety got the better of him, so he lost his counselling and eventually the benefits he was claiming.

At that time, his PTSD had been more severe, and he'd not been well enough to hold down a job. Consequently, he couldn't pay his rent or claim any housing benefits, so he lost his home, too. There were places at a couple of hostels, but they wouldn't allow him to take Bess. That's why Danny, an ex-soldier, someone who'd served his country, was sleeping out on the streets.

Even though I was wearing a winter coat and knitted sweater, I'd been so cold that first night: a typically cool one for late April in the UK. Danny offered to share his sleeping bag with me, and even though I'd declined his offer at first, by the early hours of the following day, I was so bitterly cold I finally gave in and cuddled up next to him. And I'd done so every night since.

I spent my days trying to keep out of the rain, begging with Danny in the mornings and through the busy lunchtime hours, then settling down somewhere safe with him and Bess at night.

I told him about some of my past, and he could empathise with me a little. Danny's background hadn't been all that great either, and he had no family to speak of. That's why he'd joined the army. Something positive in his life. Somewhere he'd belong and where he'd make a difference. Pity it hadn't worked out for him. Danny's a good man and deserves so much better.

I also told him about Jean's heart attack and my arrival at the children's home—shuddering at the memories that day evoked. Even as I sipped the remnants of my last hot drink of the day, thinking about my time at The Willows, and the problems Sarah and I had during our stay, brought out the same reaction.

My mother had been a drug addict who used prostitution to fund her habit. She'd often brought the men she picked up to the two-up two-down council house we had in central Doncaster, and for more years than I remember, I'd stayed hidden while they were with her.

It had been my fourteenth birthday when I went into her bedroom to stop a man from beating her. When she brought him home, I'd locked my bedroom door as usual, staying quiet in my room so that I didn't alert him to my presence. I'd heard them having sex, and I prayed he'd be one of those quick finishers who paid well, so I wouldn't have to listen to his grunting and groaning for too long. But then I'd heard a fist hitting flesh and my mother crying out in pain, followed by another blow and a scream.

I ran to my door and listened as more and more punches rained down on her, and I knew I had to stop him. So, after quietly unlocking the door, I took the cricket bat I kept by the side of it and made my way down to my mother's bedroom. I could hear the guy calling her a fucking bitch and a dirty whore while he hit her harder.

She was screaming for him to stop, and though she'd always told me I should never go to her room and interfere—no matter what I heard—when the guy said the world would be a better place if she were dead, I opened the bedroom door and ran towards him, swinging the cricket bat as hard as I could at his head.

Unfortunately for me, the man beating my mother had

quick reflexes and ducked down before the bat made contact, which caused me to fall forward. That's when he turned his fists onto *my* face and body before picking up the cricket bat and using that. I tried to shield myself with my arms and hands, but I couldn't stop the bat from connecting with what felt like every inch of my body. It seemed to go on forever, but in reality, it was only seconds before I stopped feeling the pain and hearing the noises that accompanied the violence. And just before my world turned black, I saw my mother diving towards the man's bare back with a knife in her hands.

I woke up a week later in hospital after being put in a medically induced coma. Once the swelling on my brain from the savage beating had reduced, they'd gradually brought me back to a conscious state, but they couldn't be sure if I'd have any long-term effects.

Thankfully, I hadn't suffered any brain damage, but I was still black and blue all over, with four broken ribs, a fractured cheekbone and collarbone, and three broken fingers. I had various cuts about my face that were already healing by the time they brought me out of the coma, yet they were still sore, and the cut above my eyebrow needed stitches.

The police tried to interview me, but they weren't allowed in until the social worker arrived. Her name was Andrea, and she explained what had happened after I became unconscious. My mother had stabbed the man, Philip Casey, several times, and he'd died twenty-four hours later. She'd used his phone to call the ambulance, then injected herself with a lethal dose of heroin. She died in the ambulance outside our home after several failed attempts at resuscitation.

When I heard my mother had killed herself, I felt my eyes tingle and thought I was going to cry, but due to the extreme swelling and bruising around them, no tears could form. The doctors explained the mechanics of that to me, but they couldn't explain why I didn't cry for her when I'd healed. Maybe it was because I'd expected it to happen one day anyway? She'd been a junkie for most of my life, and I'd found her near death a few times over the years. Still, you'd have thought I'd have cried for her, and the fact that I hadn't had the social workers wanting to send me to counselling. But I refused to go. I'd stopped trusting anyone in authority before the appointment came through.

I was placed in temporary foster care until they checked to see if I had any family who might come forward and take me in. I told the social worker not to hold her breath on that ever happening. I didn't know who my father was, and the only one left on my mother's side was my grandmother, who was serving time in prison for dealing Class A drugs. The look the social worker gave me when I told her was one I'd been familiar with for years… *Poor Tess, bound to end up the same way as her mother or grandmother. There's no hope for this one.*

I'd seen that look so often from my teachers, Mum's last rehab counsellor, and even Mrs Henshall in the local shop. They all expected me to follow in my family's footsteps, but I was determined that wouldn't happen. I won't ever be like them. I'll never put myself in a position where my life choices are ruled by drugs or alcohol.

The police were more abrupt when speaking to me than I'd

expected them to be. They had to be reminded by the social worker that they were speaking to a minor who'd gone through a traumatic experience and was still recovering. They'd even asked if I'd been selling my body alongside my mother.

I'd been examined while I was unconscious, so they knew I hadn't been raped and was still a virgin. I told them I'd never been involved in my mother's profession, but I could tell they didn't believe me. One of them even suggested I performed other services for men while my mother stole from them, and that's why Philip Casey had "*lashed out*."

I became angry and upset, so they made the police leave, but I knew it wouldn't be the last time I'd be accused of doing something I hadn't done.

I found ways to turn my mind blank and my expression neutral when faced with those questions because I hated the satisfied smirk they wore when they knew they'd gotten a reaction from me.

It was reported in the newspapers that Mr Philip Casey had been a hard-working man who raised money for cancer charities in his spare time. He'd been a loyal husband and doting father before that fateful night he'd been *"lured"* back to our home by my mother.

Despite my telling the police what happened, the full events of that night weren't made public until nearly eleven months later, and by that time, I was staying with my foster mother, Jean Brent.

Jean was there with me throughout the inquest and helped shield me from the reporters outside the court, as well as

Philip Casey's family. They'd spat at me a few times, calling me a murdering, junkie slut, even though I was a victim and had never even held the knife.

Jean had been my rock. She was the same with the other two girls who'd been in her care: Sarah and Christine. Sarah was two years younger than me but came from a similar background, and we became friends instantly. I wasn't as keen on Christine, the older girl. She was a bit stuck-up and believed herself better than us. She'd been in foster care because her mum had a nervous breakdown and was in the hospital. Christine had no other family who could take her in, only her grandparents. But they were elderly and in poor health, so she ended up in short-term foster care until her mum was better.

Even though Sarah and I were supposed to be staying with Jean short term, we were with her for over two years. Christine stayed less than eight weeks.

Apart from the police interviews and the inquest, the time I spent living at Jean's home was the happiest I've ever been in my life. I'd felt safe, well cared for, and loved. When Jean had her heart attack and we were taken to the children's home, all that safety and love went out of the window, and the nightmare that was my life began all over again.

Sarah and I ended up at The Willows an hour or so after they'd taken Jean away in the ambulance. She had a triple heart bypass and wasn't allowed to foster us again after her surgery and subsequent recovery, but I know she tried. She even came to visit us at The Willows until Lisa—a bitchy residential social worker—decided to put a stop to it.

2

TESS

Sarah had always been wild and reckless. Being older, I instinctively looked out for her, trying to keep her from getting into trouble. Never an easy task where Sarah was concerned.

Almost a year after we'd found ourselves at The Willows, Sarah and I began attending a youth centre about a mile away. We played basketball and other sports there after school, and on Thursdays, they had a disco.

The DJ was a tall, good-looking Asian guy of Pakistani origin called Tariq. He was fun to be around and always gave us his full attention when he spoke to us. He seemed particularly interested in Sarah and Beth, another teenage girl from The Willows.

At first, I thought he was looking out for Sarah and Beth; his influence seemed to be helping on the behavioural front. Sarah rarely got into any more fights at school and, as far as I was aware, her shoplifting habit had declined. Then one day, when we sat in the bedroom we shared, Sarah pulled an iPhone out of her pocket and began texting someone.

I asked her how she got it, knowing we would never usually get anything as good as that given through social services or The Willows, and my first thought was that she'd stolen it. Sarah laughed at my worried expression and told me it was a gift from Tariq's friend, Farid. She said he was in Tariq's car when he'd given her and Beth a lift back to The Willows. She told me he was really friendly and had asked for their mobile numbers so he could call them and take them to the travelling fair, which was coming to the next town.

When Sarah and Beth told him they didn't have mobile phones, he said he felt sorry for them, but because he liked them and wanted to be friends, he gave them both a phone from a bag he had in the boot of Tariq's car. He said he fixed and sold mobile phones, so he happened to have them going spare. Sarah and Beth were thrilled and listened eagerly while he explained how to use them.

Farid programmed a few numbers in them so they could contact him and Tariq. He'd even credited the phones with ten pounds. I remember Sarah sighing and saying how sweet and kind he was, and while not as good-looking as Tariq, his kindness and generosity more than made up for it.

I'd exhausted myself telling Sarah it was a bad idea to meet up with this Farid guy, but both she and Beth were adamant they wanted to see him again, even if it was only to thank him for the phones.

As promised, he picked them up and took them to a travelling fair in Conisborough.

Sarah returned late that night, happier than I'd seen her since we lived at Jean's house. Farid and two of his friends treated her and Beth to a go on every ride at the fair, and each had an armful of soft toys the men had won for them.

Sarah told them how much she hated being at The Willows and how she'd loved living with Jean. She'd also mentioned I was worried about her meeting them. They'd told her to bring me with her next time, so I could see they were only trying to be friends. I declined that invitation and every other one they offered over the next few weeks.

Farid and another guy named Hassan spoiled Sarah and Beth with gifts of clothing and CDs. I watched helplessly while my only friend drifted away from me as she fell in love with both Farid and the new lifestyle she was living.

Nine weeks after she first met Farid, Sarah came to me, heartbroken. She'd cried for an hour before she told me what had happened. She'd been having sex with Farid at least twice a week for the last couple of weeks, but now he said that because he loved her—and was proud of how sexy she was—he wanted to show her off to his friends.

She went with him to a house about an hour's drive away in the Nottingham area—from what she could gather by the road signs. When they got inside, there were at least seven other men waiting for them. Beth and Hassan were already there, and Hassan asked if Beth would kiss some of the other men—which she did. But when Farid asked Sarah, she refused.

Farid hadn't expected her refusal. He told her if she loved him, she would do it.

Sarah refused again.

Farid became angry. He'd said if she wasn't willing to do it, it would mean she didn't love him, so he'd have to dump her. Sarah had cried and begged him not to, but he hadn't backed down. He told Sarah that if she didn't show him how much she wanted to be with him by kissing those men, then that would be the end, and he'd have to take back the phone and all the other things he'd bought her.

So, to make Farid happy, Sarah kissed all the other men in that room. They didn't only kiss her, though; they touched her while they masturbated over her too. When they were done, she told me Farid came to her and held her tightly, telling her how much he loved her and how thrilled he was that she was his girlfriend. He said it made him happy that his friends found her so sexy. But Sarah felt disgusted by what they'd done. She was upset and confused about Farid allowing his friends to *do that* to her.

We talked well into the night, and Sarah came to a decision: she was going to tell Farid it was over.

But Sarah didn't give Farid his marching orders, and she confided in me less and less as time went on. I also began noticing certain changes in her. Sarah's thick and glossy hair became lank and greasy, and her deep-blue eyes looked glazed and lifeless.

I suspected drugs. My mother had been an addict for most of my life, so I knew the signs. When I asked Sarah if she was using drugs, she started screaming at me, saying I knew nothing about her and should keep my nose out of her business. She said I was jealous because she had a boyfriend who loved her. I pointed out that boyfriends shouldn't want their girlfriends kissing other men.

Sarah began yelling all kinds of nonsense, which ended with—by having sex with her boyfriend's friends, she was showing him she loved him. Then she'd stormed off in a rage, but I knew if I didn't report the matter, Sarah could be in real danger.

I didn't trust any of the staff at The Willows; I hated nearly every one of them for their uncaring attitude and complete indifference to our welfare. So, without further delay, I told one of the teachers at school instead.

There'd already been concerns about Sarah's continuing truancy and lack of effort whilst in lessons, which I was aware of from overhearing a telephone conversation with a social worker. But as Sarah was younger than me, she wasn't in the same school year, so I wasn't aware of how bad it had become.

The female teacher I'd told of my concerns was Mrs Keating, who immediately rang the police and social services. They pulled Sarah out of her lessons and brought her to the head's office. That was the last I saw of her for a few days. She was taken away and temporarily placed elsewhere.

Five days later, Sarah was brought back to The Willows. She looked much cleaner and healthier, and I hoped the change would continue.

That night, when it was time for bed, I expected some soul searching or anger from her. What I heard instead was something far worse.

I entered our room and found an anxious-looking Sarah

sitting on the end of my bed, wringing her hands together, so I instantly went to sit beside her. She took a deep, hesitant breath before saying, "I've told the police you were telling lies, Tess. I said you were jealous of me, and because I'm best friends with Beth, you hate it. I said you made up that stuff because you didn't want me to be friends with anyone but you."

I asked her why she'd lied, and what she told me made my blood run cold. Farid and Hassan had stated if she ever told the authorities what happened at the houses they took her to, they would hurt me and Jean.

From their phones, they'd shown her photos of Jean as she got into the car outside her house, so they knew where she lived. They then showed her photographs of me waiting for the school bus and walking out of the library. Farid had remarked it'd be such a shame to see Jean's house burning down during the night while she slept, and he told her it would be easy to kidnap me and take me to one of their houses, strip me naked and tie me to a bed.

She insisted everything would work out okay, anyway, because, although the other men used condoms with her, Farid hadn't because she was on the pill. But Sarah hadn't been taking it. She'd been trying to get pregnant so that Farid wouldn't share her anymore.

I shook my head, knowing how wrong she was, but Sarah insisted she knew what she was doing. By getting pregnant, she said it would keep Jean and me safe, and Farid would probably want to marry her. I tried everything I could to reason with Sarah, but it came to nothing as usual. A determined Sarah could not be stopped, so I let it go, cuddled up close to her, and tried my best to sleep that night.

We caught the bus together in a rush the next morning after oversleeping, and the last I saw of her was when she went the opposite direction down the school corridor towards her classroom.

When Sarah didn't come home with me from school, I wasn't worried. More often than not, she had detention and was kept behind, so she would miss the bus. But when she didn't come home at all that night, I began to get really anxious.

In the months since Sarah first met Farid, she'd regularly rolled in around 2 a.m. after sneaking out—although rarely unnoticed—down the fire escape. So, as per usual, I waited up for her. But Sarah didn't return. At 3 a.m., one of the social workers came into the room and asked if I knew where she was, but there was nothing I could tell them. I was as clueless as they were. At 4 a.m. I'd heard a bleeping that turned out to be her iPhone, which was running out of battery. I got up and found the charger and plugged it in. It struck me as odd that she'd gone without her phone; Sarah rarely went anywhere without it. Then I remembered we'd overslept and had left in a hurry.

I scrolled through her messages, and the last one received was from Farid. It read, *"will pick u up @ 11 a.m. next 2 school bus stop and take u 2 McDs."*

There were other messages on there with other pickup places, and some that said, *"don't b sad, u no I luv u."*

I flicked through her photos and saw numerous pics of

Farid and her together, of Beth and who I assumed to be Hassan, along with one or two of Tariq. If she didn't come home, I knew what I would do. I'd take the phone to Jean, and we'd go to the police together. I didn't want either of their threats against us to happen, but I wanted my foster sister safe and sound.

The next day, I took the phone and charger with me to school and kept it in the bottom of my blazer where the lining had ripped, and that's where it stayed all day.

Leaving school, I'd walked amongst a crowd of loud sixth formers, and I noticed a silver car parked where the bus normally pulled in. Being seventeen, I only had a few months left at school to finish my A levels, and on that particular day, my schoolbag had been heavy with files and books. My slender five-foot-four frame had struggled with the weight of them as I sank further into the crowd.

Some of the lads in my sixth form class were almost six feet in height, and when they noticed the car, they began banging on the windows and roof. It wasn't until one of them shouted *"PAKIS,"* before banging even harder, that I glanced inside, wanting to apologise for their racial slur.

But there, in the passenger seat, sat Hassan, and driving the car was Farid.

I froze, staring right at them until Hassan made his hand and fingers into a gun shape that he pointed straight at me. He made it as if he pulled an imaginary trigger, then laughed as Farid drove the car away.

My breath caught in my throat, and I felt the hairs bristle on the back of my neck as fear took over me. Luckily the bus came, so I got on it as quickly as I could. As it was a double-decker, I ran to the upstairs level. From there, I knew I'd have a better vantage point to see if the car was following the bus.

I didn't spot the car again, so I got off at the stop across from The Willows and ran as quickly as I could over the road, narrowly escaping being run over by a guy on a moped.

I made it inside without further incident, but before I could do or say anything, Beth grabbed my shoulder and pushed me against the door.

"Where's Sarah's phone?" she spat as she pulled my schoolbag from my shoulder, tipping the contents onto the floor in the hallway.

I told her I didn't have it, so she slapped my face, then thrust her hands inside my school blazer, searching the internal pockets for the phone. I grabbed her hair and pulled her to the floor before I punched her in the nose and screamed, "Where is she?"

I carried on punching her until I was pulled away by Lisa and Ben, two of the residential social workers. Beth leapt to her feet, but before she ran out of the door, she made a gun shape with her hand and said, "Hassan says he's coming for you."

Lisa and Ben tried questioning me about the fight, and about Sarah's whereabouts, but I screamed at them to let me go. They'd already been told about Sarah's problems before she went missing, and that had gone nowhere.

Lisa shouted up the stairs as I ran to my room, informing me that the police were coming to speak to me about Sarah, so I wasn't to go anywhere. I knew after Beth's threat that telling them anything would be a risk to Jean—if I couldn't get her to leave the area first—and I was torn about what I should do.

I changed out of my school uniform, dressing hurriedly in jeans and a long-sleeved top. Because I couldn't seem to get myself warm, I put on my thickest sweater—one that Jean had bought me when I lived with her.

I went to the window and looked over at the road outside, immediately spotting a silver car parked on the side street adjacent to The Willows. I didn't need to see its occupants to know who they were.

I was hungry, but I didn't want to chance going downstairs in case Beth had come back. If she accused me of stealing Sarah's phone in front of anyone, I'd get into even more trouble.

Because the phone held photographs of Sarah and Farid together, if Sarah didn't return soon, I knew the police would need to see it. So I couldn't risk Beth getting her hands on it.

After about thirty minutes, the silver car drove away; when I saw the police car pull into the driveway, I knew why. But it was the vehicle following the police car that captured my attention. I watched as the occupants got out and looked up towards The Willows' front door. One of them was that bloody detective who'd accused me of being involved in my mother's profession and the death of Philip Casey.

I realised then I couldn't stay and speak to them. They wouldn't believe what I had to say, anyway. So I quickly threw some clothes and underwear into my backpack—along with the iPhone charger—then I lifted the carpet underneath my bedside drawers and took out the money I'd been saving.

It was only around sixty-five pounds, but it was better than nothing. I'd earned it by doing the odd bit of gardening and other errands for Jean's neighbours.

Stuffing the money in one pocket and the iPhone in the other, I took one more look out of the window.

The silver car hadn't come back.

There was a knock on the bedroom door and Ben shouted, "Tess, the police are here." I shouted back, telling him I needed a few minutes to get dressed as I'd just got out of the shower. Ben told me to come straight down to the office when I was done, so I said I would.

I waited until I heard his footsteps descending the stairs, then made my way back to the window.

The windows were alarmed but not locked because of fire regulations. Sarah had cut through the wires weeks ago so she could come up the fire escape and through the bedroom window when she'd been out late with Farid.

I gently opened the window and placed my backpack on the fire escape steps. Then I made my way out the window as quietly as possible—which was hard to do while wearing my hooded winter coat. Still trying to make as little noise as possible, I hurried down the metal fire escape.

Keeping the hood up on my padded green parka to disguise my distinctive copper-coloured curly hair, I ran swiftly across the garden, climbing awkwardly over the wall onto the street.

As luck would have it, a bus was just pulling up to the stop, so I got on it, not even caring where it went. The bus took me all the way to Doncaster's bus and rail interchange, then I made my way from the bus station over to the train station.

I wasn't sure where I was headed but knew I had to get as far away as possible. There was a train due to leave the station for London's King's Cross, so I made a split-second decision that was where I should go.

I couldn't afford a ticket, but I jumped on the train anyway, managing to avoid the conductor by spending nearly all the journey in the surprisingly clean toilet cubicle, slipping out just moments after we entered King's Cross Station.

So that's how I found myself sleeping rough in London. Rather that than fall into the hands of Hassan and Farid.

3

TESS

After drinking the last of my hot chocolate, I went to throw the Styrofoam cup in a nearby bin. Glancing to my left, I saw someone who made me freeze in my tracks.

It was Tariq.

He kept his eyes on me, lifting his mobile phone to his ear as he began walking in my direction. I quickly scanned the surrounding area, trying to get back to where I'd left Danny and Bess, but when I rounded the corner, I spotted Farid heading directly for me.

Panicking, I turned to my right, running towards a crowd of people making their way from the financial district. I darted past the suited men and women as fast as I could before pausing in a doorway to catch my breath.

I glanced to my left, then right, making sure I wasn't being followed before stepping back out onto the pavement. It was much quieter and less crowded on this end of the street, and I found myself nervously looking for any Asian guys on mobile phones.

While glancing around, I noticed a man with his right hand slipping into his jacket and staying there. Although he had a similar skin tone and dark hair, he didn't quite fit the bill of the men who were hunting me down. Nevertheless, something just didn't seem right about him, and I had a gut feeling that something bad was about to happen.

The door I'd previously been standing against opened, revealing five men in suits who made their way towards a waiting vehicle.

As if in slow motion, the guy with his hand in his jacket pulled out a gun, aiming it at one of the five men. Without thinking of the consequences, I ran the few steps needed to reach them, leaping up to pull the man the gun was directly aimed at out of harm's way. I heard a loud crack and felt a sharp, burning pain below my collarbone before being grabbed and pulled to the ground, the man I'd just saved covering my body with his while chaos erupted all around us.

I heard shouting and two more loud noises—unmistakably gunfire—coming from men beside me this time. I cried out in pain, hearing someone barking orders and the squeal of tyres as a car sped away. The man covering me said something I couldn't comprehend as agonising pain and fear dulled my senses. The pain expanded throughout my upper body when he picked me up and placed me inside the back of a vehicle.

4

TESS

I knew I should ask where I was being taken, but I couldn't seem to speak—my words swallowed by the searing pain below my collarbone. All that registered in my pain-filled haze was the gentle stroking of my hair and calming words, some in English and others in a foreign language I didn't recognise.

I looked up to find the most beautiful blue eyes I'd ever seen gazing down at me. The man holding me—the man I'd prevented being shot—was telling me everything would be okay. He told me he was taking me to a private hospital, where he had one of the best surgeons in the capital awaiting my arrival.

The blue-eyed man said his name was Kolya Barinov, and he owed me his life. He asked me my name and if I could give him some information so he could contact my family. But I shook my head at that question, causing more pain to radiate down my body, making me cry out in agony. The pain worsened when he carried me from the vehicle and placed me on a hospital trolley. A waiting team of men and women in blue scrubs swarmed around me, wheeling me briskly along a corridor to a brightly lit room.

A nurse asked me my name and if I had allergies, and in a croaky voice, I answered, "No allergies."

The blue-eyed man held my hand until he was forced to let go when a man in scrubs began cutting away my clothing. An oxygen mask was placed over my mouth and nose, cutting off my protest. Then a female voice said, "*Sharp scratch*," and I immediately felt myself go woozy before the pain dulled a little.

There was a familiar tightening on my upper arm when a blood pressure monitor inflated a cuff they'd attached to it at some point, and a machine beeped continuously, which I found reassuring. Each of those beeps meant I was still alive.

Someone was barking orders at the busy hospital staff, but I couldn't comprehend the words.

A doctor pressed the area around the bullet wound, causing me to cry out in agony before begging him to stop. I tried to pull the mask away from my mouth, but I could barely lift my arms. Someone shouted, *"Straight to theatre three and page Mr Grayson,"* before wheeling me down another brightly lit corridor. I noticed the man, Kolya, by my left side, following me. His cheek was smeared with blood, and his shirt and suit jacket were saturated with it.

My blood! I had lost so much—I could see that clearly—and worried I might not survive the surgery.

Kolya grabbed my hand as they wheeled me through a set of double doors. Although he smiled at me in reassurance, I could see the fear in his ice-blue eyes. Despite my own fear, I smiled back at him, gripping his fingers until he was ushered away and the doors closed.

5

KOLYA

I don't know how long I'd been staring at those closed doors, but it felt like hours. My hands were shaking, and breathing had become a much harder task. Fearing that this waif of a woman may not survive caused a crushing band to form around my chest. My hands, jacket, shirt and tie were covered in her blood, the metallic tang of it saturating the air.

"Would you like to take a seat in the waiting area, sir?" a nurse asked before taking my arm and guiding me to a room next to the theatre doors. My feet seemed rooted to the spot where her hand slipped from mine as they'd wheeled her away, and it took a few seconds for me to move freely.

"Can I get anyone a cup of tea or coffee?" the nurse enquired.

Anyone?

I looked around and noticed four of my guards following me into the room. Jonesy, Nate and Lucas took a seat while

Ivan stood guard at the door. When the nurse left to get our drinks, I turned to my guards and asked, "Can anyone tell me what the fuck just happened?"

"Boss, we shouldn't have let Mr Markos's guards handle security. It's a new team. We haven't worked with them before. Jonesy and Nate warned you against letting them carry out pre-exit recon and lead security before we left," Lucas said bitterly.

The others all voiced their agreement. Not many people in my position would let their staff speak to them so informally, but that was how I chose to run my business. I trusted my security, and yes, both Nate and Jonesy had told me they weren't happy with letting Yannis's new security detail lead. My friend had scoffed at their concerns and had queried whether I trusted his ability to keep us safe.

Yannis Markos and I have been the greatest of friends since we met at Oxford University almost twenty-three years ago. Both he and I, along with Chen Yu and Imran Barhi, had bonded immediately. Probably because we were the only foreign students on our course that year. But it was with Yannis I'd spent most of my time as I made my way through my university years.

Yannis had introduced me to my late wife, which was one of the reasons why Catherine had wanted him to be our son's godfather.

We've spent so many holidays together over the years, and my son thinks of him as family. We've often gone out when staying with him in Greece or on the island he owns—with only his security to guard us. I'd never once questioned that he wouldn't keep us safe then. So why start now?

Obviously, his new staff did not deserve the confidence he'd had in their abilities. Yet there was no guarantee, even with the highest level of security, that someone who was really out to get you could not do so out in public.

"The shooter… Do we have any information? Or did he manage to get away?" I asked.

I'd heard further gunfire while I was down on the pavement, shielding the wounded young woman with my body—desperate to protect the stranger who had almost given her life to save mine.

"Franco fired a couple of shots, both hit him in the upper back, but although he dropped to the ground, he got up and jumped into the back of a vehicle. Kevin has the details," replied Lucas.

"So, the shooter wore a Kevlar vest and came with backup? I doubt we'll get anywhere with vehicle details. Did Kevin carry out my orders for a swipe and wipe of all nearby CCTV footage?" I didn't want the police interfering if one of my men had fired a shot. It's against the law in Britain to carry handguns.

"Kevin hacked the systems of each of the surrounding buildings within five minutes of receiving your order, as well as local authority surveillance. All nearby CCTV cameras were too far away to pick up any of the shots fired, but they should give us a clear picture of the driver at least. As far as we're aware, there were two calls to police reporting suspected gunfire, but we were gone by the time they arrived," Jonesy informed me.

"Good! Ask him to run the shooter through the facial recognition programme he has."

"Kevin said he and Steve are searching through each of the buildings' camera footage to find the clearest frame of his facial features, then he'll run them through the programme." Jonesy paused for a moment before saying what we were all thinking. "What that man can't do with a computer wouldn't cover the back of an eyelash."

We all nodded as a smile emerged on Nate's face.

Nate and Kevin have been a couple for almost four years. Nate works for me in close protection, while Kevin oversees the technical side of my security. A job he does extremely well. The man is a technological genius and well worth the seven-figure salary I pay him.

My phone was once again vibrating in my pocket; it had done so ever since we'd bundled the young woman into the car. The bullet had torn through her shoulder, just below her collarbone. It would have taken too long for an ambulance to arrive in the heavy London traffic, so I'd given my team orders to bring her to the private hospital where my squash partner was a surgeon.

"I'm sorry I didn't listen to your warning, Nate, Jonesy," I said, nodding to both of them. "If I had, that poor, innocent young woman wouldn't be fighting for her life on an operating table right now."

"I'm sure she'll be fine, boss," Jonesy assured me in his strong Welsh accent.

"She was hit in the same place as Franco was when we were out on patrol in Helmand Hellhole," Nate muttered. "Took us over an hour to get him to the surgeon back at base, and he recovered pretty damn quick. We got her here within eight minutes, so she'll be fine, boss; just wait and see."

"But she lost so much blood!" I gestured at the deep red staining my clothes. No one said anything for a moment, though the air was heavy with unspoken worry.

"Did you catch her name?" asked Nate.

"She would not give it, nor would she tell me who to contact. The medical team also asked her, but she wouldn't answer."

"Perhaps she has no one," Ivan remarked from his position by the door. Nate, Jonesy, and Lucas frowned, then looked towards me.

"If it was true before, it isn't now. The young woman is under my protection until she requests otherwise or if her loved ones come to claim her. She saved my life. I will see that she is rewarded."

"She had a backpack with her. It's still in the car. Maybe there'll be something in it with her name and address," Lucas suggested.

A nurse came into the room wheeling a trolley laden with tea, coffee, and biscuits. Before she left, she pointed out where I could shower and change. A not-so-subtle hint to get me to remove my bloodstained clothing from the comfortable fabric chairs.

I put a call through to my PA to request a change of clothes be brought to the hospital before listening to the numerous messages from Yannis, apologising for the failure of his guards to secure the area before we left the building. He asked me to call him back to let him know how I was, if I knew the red-headed woman who leapt into the line of fire to save me, and if I had any information about the shooter.

I did not call him back.

As yet, I had nothing to tell him. Not about the woman or the shooter. And I did not want to let him off the hook so easily regarding the epic failure of his security detail. A failure that could have cost me my life. One that nearly cost the life of a red-headed, amber-eyed angel who'd just made sure my son had at least one of his parents still alive.

6

TESS

Couldn't someone switch off that bloody machine? I so desperately needed to sleep, but the stupid bleeping from the ever-inflating blood pressure monitor was all I could hear until someone shuffled beside me.

Looking towards the shuffling noise, I found the blue-eyed man. After a few moments, I recalled his name. Kolya! Yes, that was it. And he was sitting in a chair by the side of my bed.

"Hello, little one," he said, running the back of his fingers over my cheek. "It's good to see you awake at last. Keep still a moment; I've just pressed for the nurse."

Within seconds of him saying that, a grey-haired nurse in a mid-blue uniform appeared, standing to the right of my bed.

"Well, young lady, it's good to see you awake. My name is Maria, and I'll be your nurse for the next few hours until I leave for the night. So if there's anything you need, just press the button on this little device." She took the call button from Kolya and placed it in my hand.

"Would you like a sip of water?" she asked while taking my temperature with one of those in-ear thermometers. I nodded my head. She grabbed a chart and began marking down my temperature and blood pressure readings, which were illuminated on the constantly inflating machine. When she'd finished with her paperwork, Nurse Maria picked up a cup with a straw in it and brought it towards my mouth. I stupidly tried to lift my head, wincing when pain radiated through my neck and shoulder.

"Now, now, *malyutka*. Be still. Let us bring the water to you," Kolya commanded, taking the cup and straw away from her and then bringing it to my lips. I'd taken three sips before Nurse Maria said that was enough for now, and the cup was taken away.

To my utter relief, she switched off the blood pressure machine and removed the cuff.

"We don't seem to have your details, so I'll need you to give me some information so we can update your medical records. Let's start with your name, shall we?" she asked, reaching for yet more paperwork.

I shook my head and lowered my eyes to avoid her gaze. No way would I give her my name. I wasn't about to let Tariq and the rest of them find out which hospital I was at so they could get to me in my weakened state.

"Thank you, Maria, that will be all for now," said Kolya. I avoided Maria's eyes as she flicked at the steady drip that was attached to a cannula in my arm.

When she left the room, Kolya spoke.

"Look at me, *malyutka*. Whatever you are running from, you need to know I'll protect you. You saved my life today; therefore, I owe you a good life in return. You are in a private hospital in London, which doesn't usually take emergency cases or offer no-questions-asked surgery. But I am a very wealthy man, and that wealth buys silence, as well as the best medical care. Your details will be kept private and used only to research your past medical history, so they can determine the best possible treatment. So tell me, *malyutka*, what is your name?"

"What does *malyutka* mean?" I asked. He'd called me that several times and I hadn't a clue what it meant.

"It means little one. You seem so small and delicate, yet you threw yourself in front of an assassin's bullet to save the life of someone you didn't know. Your strength and bravery belie your stature and obvious youth."

I sighed and closed my eyes. I didn't want to be brave. In my world, bravery had only ever brought me pain and suffering, but I seemed to have an inbuilt need to save people. It was an annoyingly painful habit I needed to kick as soon as possible before I got myself killed.

"Tell me your name and why you don't want anyone else to know. I promise I will keep you safe."

"Safe?" I questioned. The word held no meaning to me. I had never felt truly safe in my whole life—apart from when I lived with Jean.

"How can you keep me safe? Someone shot at you. Why

did they do that?" A valid question, I thought, under the circumstances.

Kolya leaned forward and held my hand for a moment before kissing my fingers. Then he sat back in his chair and captured my gaze with those ice-blue eyes, still holding my hand, his thumb gently brushing over the back of my fingers.

"Let me introduce myself properly, *malyutka*. As you know, my name is Kolya Barinov, and I'm an extremely successful businessman. My company has offices, laboratories, testing, and build sites in the UK, Russia, Germany, China, and America. My business both creates and distributes weaponry to various companies and armed forces in many countries. All of that could make me a target for a number of reasons."

He carried on speaking when I didn't reply to what he'd just told me.

"I was born just outside of Moscow and came to England when I was eighteen to study engineering at Oxford University. As a young teenager in Russia, I was fascinated with weapons and their mechanisms, and due to my father's line of work, I'd been around guns and ammunition from a very young age, which helped fuel my interest. I have two older brothers who followed my father in business, so I was left to do as I pleased regarding my education and career. I studied chemistry and physics, using the knowledge I gained to help me further understand weaponry and ammunition and what they needed to make them more effective.

"I finished my course a year earlier than I should have,

then began studying engineering. I learned that to understand what made a good weapon, you had to know everything about it—from the materials used to build it, the way it was designed, and what type of ammunition would be most effective to serve its purpose. My examination results were excellent, and I secured a place at Oxford University. So, I travelled to England and earned my degree in engineering, continuing my education throughout the following three years by further study of physics and chemistry."

Kolya gave me a smile that reached those ice-blue eyes and made him seem less intimidating.

"I was a bit of a geek, as you younger ones would say. At sixteen, I inherited a substantial amount of money from my grandfather's estate—as did each of my brothers. As well as taking advice on other ways to invest, I bought a failing weaponry business in Russia. I also set up a similar one here in the UK. It was a good job the investments I made in the gas expansion pipelines paid off. My weaponry business made nothing for two years," he added.

"I met my wife at a party when I was nineteen. I fell in love with her from that very first moment, and the time I should have spent investing in my business and university studies was spent with her instead. By twenty-one, I was married, had a son, and was just finishing my degree, trying my best to keep two failing businesses afloat. Something had to give, and for the next three years, I spent most of my waking moments committed to getting my business up and running.

"Working with my team of scientists and engineers, I

created a formula and design for a long-range missile that was more accurate in its targeting than any on the market. I thought it would take forever to pitch the weapon to any kind of buyer, but the world was still reeling from the First Gulf War, and both the Saudis and Iranians made a play for it.

"A good friend I studied with at Oxford had gone back home to China to work in the family business—manufacturing steel and other metals. I made a deal with him that his company would supply the hard materials and produce the larger components. After my first successful sale, I was inundated with offers from several other countries, but the largest bid came from the USA."

Kolya gave an unmissable smirk, and I could see he relished telling me the next part of his story.

"In addition to the US Department of Defence wanting the weapon, they also offered a contract for a factory, lab, and warehousing. And a substantial financial reward if I committed to providing them with this weapon and another two in my company's portfolio. The deal was they'd have exclusivity for up to five years with one of the new weapons. After much legal debating and a larger financial settlement, I finally agreed to their terms, and we began production six months later near Seattle. I changed the name of the business from Barinov to KOLCAT Engineering, as tensions were still high regarding anyone from the former Soviet Union in the US. My son is studying over there now. He will take over the American side of the business when he finishes his education and is competent enough."

"So, you have a wife and son," I stated. "They must have

been worried when they heard someone attempted to shoot you."

Kolya got up and walked towards the window. He didn't say anything for a few moments—like he'd forgotten I was even in the room.

"Catherine, my wife, died in a riding accident eight years ago. She was crazy about show jumping and was very adept at the sport. But she had a reckless streak, too, and was thrown from her horse while trying to jump a gate near our home. She broke her neck on impact with the hard, frosty ground and died three days later. She shouldn't have been out riding on her own and without head protection, but you could never tell Catherine what to do. I was back in Russia on business, and it was hours before I got to see her. Our son was just eleven years old. She had been everything to him, and to me.

"They'd both followed me around the world for a time when I conducted business, but as my company grew more successful, the risk to them while travelling with me increased. In the two years before her death, both Catherine and my son, James, had stayed in England whenever I went away on business.

"My wife's father was James Lassiter, owner of the Lassiter Hotel Group. Catherine had been busy dealing with lawyers regarding her father's estate; he'd passed away and left her as the sole heir to his company. She hadn't wanted to deal with all of it while still grieving. I should have been there to help her. I should…"

I didn't offer him comfort, even though I could see these

revelations pained him. Instead, I drew in a breath and began with, “My name is Tess Robertson.”

7

TESS

After I'd told Kolya all about myself and my life so far, I expected the same look that everyone other than Jean, Danny, and Sarah had given me. The one that said I was doomed to fail in life and would never amount to anything good. Instead, all I got from Kolya was concern and questions about Tariq, Farid, and Hassan.

He wanted to know if anyone else knew where I was, and if they could have followed me to the train station. As far as I was aware, I hadn't been followed. But Tariq had known exactly where to find me in our capital city, which couldn't have been an effortless task. It was something I began to worry about with each question Kolya asked.

Before I could say anything else, he exclaimed, "The phone!" Then hastily retrieved it from my backpack.

"I saw the phone when I went through your things to try to find your information when you were in surgery. The doctors wanted to know if you had any allergies, but there was nothing personal in your backpack—other than the iPhone. I thought it was strange that the pictures on here weren't of you. Most young people are into taking selfies and such, but there were no pictures of you, just these dark-haired girls and these men," Kolya remarked as he flicked through all the photos that were stored on the device.

"The photos are of Sarah and Farid, but there's also a few of Beth, Hassan, and Tariq on there, too." I wasn't happy that he'd been rooting through my things, but I understood why he'd done it. He kept flicking through the phone, then looked up at me.

"I think it's possible these men found you because they could track the phone through GPS. Which means they know you are here at this very moment," Kolya exclaimed. He got up from the chair and swiftly made his way to the door.

I sat up a little too quickly, forgetting the shoulder wound in my panic to leave. Kolya dashed from the open door back to me when I cried out in pain, easing me back down onto the pillows gently.

"Tess, *milaya moya*, what are you doing? You must lie still and allow yourself to heal. You will hurt yourself if you try to get out of bed so quickly."

"But you don't understand, Kolya. If they find me, they'll hurt me even more than I'm hurting now. I need to leave and hide somewhere. Please, let me get up," I begged while using my legs to push me further up the bed. Kolya pinned my knees to the bed to stop me from moving.

"Listen to me, *malyutka*. You are not going anywhere until

you are well enough. I will keep you safe, you have my word on that. I will never let you come to any harm while you are in my care. Do you understand me, Tess?" He stared into my eyes, still holding down my knees until I finally lay still and compliant.

"Now, little one, will you keep still if I let you go? Two of my guards have just entered the room, and I need to speak with them about my suspicions regarding the phone. I want you to know what our plans are so you can stop worrying about hiding yourself away. I need to have your trust and cooperation in this so I can keep you safe. Do I have that, Tess? Do you trust that I will keep you safe?"

I looked at his guards, who were standing at the foot of my bed, then back to those beguiling blue eyes. I could feel the strength and power emanating from him, and not just from his tall, muscular frame. It was like it was built into him. Part of his nature, if you will. His high cheekbones and strong, bearded jaw were set in a way that spoke of determination, and I knew I could do nothing but comply with this man.

I took a deep, steadying breath, taking in the scent of his cologne and, well, him, I suppose, and it soothed me in a way I had never experienced before. So I closed my eyes and nodded my head, agreeing to his request. Seconds later, Kolya let go of my knees and picked up my hand, kissing my fingers before smiling at me.

"Thank you, Tess, for giving me your trust. Know that everyone in this room would give their life for yours without hesitation."

I glanced at the men standing solidly behind Kolya, who nodded their heads in agreement. It was a surreal moment.

It's not every day that complete strangers offer to give up their life to save yours, and if I'm honest, I wasn't comfortable with it at all. But I kept my mouth shut while Kolya explained a little of my past to them. Once again, I didn't see any judgement regarding my background, only blatant contempt for the men who were intent on finding me.

The guards' names were Franco and Nate, and both had an American accent. Both were tall, around six feet in height, and were quite muscular. Nate's dark brown skin stood out in stark contrast against his crisp white shirt, and he sported a military-style buzz cut. Although his height and stature were imposing, his eyes expressed a kindness that I was sure wasn't only reserved for injured runaways in their hour of need. Franco, on the other hand, although tall, dark, and handsome with an Italian look about him, had a fire to his chestnut-brown eyes. Like he was ready to fight at a moment's notice and welcomed danger. Although this may have made others wary of him, I felt an affinity with this man. Maybe he had a similar start in life to me and Danny?

I wondered about Danny. I knew he'd be worried about me. He'd proven to be a good friend in the short time I'd known him, and I wanted to let him know what had happened to me. I'd told Kolya all about Danny and how he'd kept me safe and warm while sleeping rough on those cold London streets.

"Kolya, I need to get a message to Danny. He'll be worried

about me. I don't want him to be out there looking for me. He doesn't need the stress."

Kolya nodded and got Nate to write down a description of Danny, Bess, and the sleeping bag. I told him where Danny preferred to sleep and on what days so they could narrow down his whereabouts. After thanking him for his help, I waited to hear what they'd decided to do about the phone, Farid, and the others.

"We can take the phone to my hotel and wait for them to arrive. Of course, they are probably already in the vicinity of this building as the phone has been here unmoving for a while. I propose we keep a guard here in your room and one outside the door. I will circulate the photographs from the phone to everyone on my staff and post a guard at the front entrance of the hospital. My team will intercept them if they try to make contact. Hopefully, they will follow me back to the hotel, then I can deal with them in familiar surroundings. Our priority is to stop them from getting to you, Tess, but I would also like to question them regarding your friend's disappearance." I could see in Kolya's eyes he didn't think they'd find Sarah, but I appreciated him trying.

He decided that Nate would stay with me in my room, and someone called Ivan would stand guard outside my door. A man named Jonesy would keep watch at the hospital entrance, and Franco and someone called Lucas would go back to Kolya's hotel with him.

Kolya circulated the photographs from Sarah's phone and then went to speak with the doctor before he left the building.

8

TESS

When Kolya and Franco left the room, Nate came over to the chair at the side of the bed and asked if I minded if he sat for a while. I shook my head and watched as he sat down and made himself comfortable. He looked at me and smiled, and although I was a little wary of being this close to a stranger, I smiled back at him. Neither of us spoke for a while. We just stared at each other—both of us assessing one another in a way. Then Nate broke the silence by exclaiming, "You are one special young lady, Tess, to take a bullet for a stranger. A real hero!"

"I'm not a hero," I told him truthfully. "I only went to push Kolya to safety, not to take a bullet."

"But you must have considered the risk?" he questioned.

"It happened so quickly; there wasn't time to consider anything." I wasn't lying. It had happened so fast, and all I could think of at the time was to push Kolya out of the way, not for the guy to shoot me instead.

"I can't believe he kept us at the rear when he left the building. We wouldn't normally do that; it's not procedure. But the boss—Mr Barinov—allowed Mr Markos's guards to go out front and give lead protection detail. It's fu…I mean, it shouldn't have happened. I assume Mr Markos will fire whoever went out first to secure the area, and I know Mr Barinov will never put himself in that situation again."

"Who's Mr Markos?" I asked.

"He's a close friend of Mr Barinov. They often spend time together socially, so I know the boss trusts Mr Markos's usual guards. Hell, we all know his usual team pretty well after all this time. But I just keep thinking if one of us had taken lead protection, then you wouldn't be lying hurt in that bed right now."

"Don't feel guilty, Nate," I told him. "At least I'm still here, and I honestly don't know what would've happened if Tariq had caught up with me. They say things happen for a reason, so maybe this was a *divine intervention,* albeit a painful one," I said, wincing as I tried to make myself more comfortable.

"Tess, are you in pain? Do you want me to get the nurse for you?" Nate asked as he leaned over the bed. I shook my head, which made the pain even worse.

"Keep still, girl, just until the nurse arrives," Nate ordered, taking the buzzer out of my hand and pressing it firmly. About a minute later, Nurse Maria came through the door, and Nate told her I was in pain. She set the blood pressure machine going, took my temperature, and then clipped something on the end of my finger before saying she'd be back in a moment. Nate pulled the chair nearer to the bed and took my hand in his until the nurse came back.

"Miss Robertson, the doctor has prescribed morphine and something to prevent nausea, which I am going to administer through your cannula. You may start to feel sleepy, so try to get some rest while you can."

I felt the effects of the drugs almost immediately, as a kind of detached feeling came over me. My weary eyes wandered over to Nate, and the concerned look on his face had me reaching for his hand again. I don't know if my hand made contact, though, because a strange calmness pulled me under, and my eyes closed.

I awoke sometime later to find Nate gone and Kolya once again sitting in the chair at the side of my bed. The clock on the wall told me it was just after two. As the curtains were closed and the room was in semi-darkness—other than the dim glow from the nightlight above my bed—I assumed it was two in the morning.

Kolya's eyes were closed, and his head was tilted back. I took a moment to look at him while he slept, taking in his appearance.

Kolya was gorgeous. There was no getting away from that. I assumed he must be about forty years old, from what he'd told me earlier. But apart from a few grey hairs appearing through the brown at his temples, you really couldn't tell. He had a short, neatly trimmed beard that suited his strong jawline and added to his blatant masculinity.

I felt bad that he wasn't sleeping in a comfortable bed, but I was also glad he was here.

Kolya appeared to care about my welfare. It wasn't what I was used to, and I appreciated his presence in what would otherwise have been a very lonely experience for me.

The door to my room opened, and in walked a different nurse. This woke Kolya, and I watched as he stretched and yawned. I glanced back at the nurse and caught her giving him an appreciative look. I couldn't blame her, but I was uncomfortable with it, too.

"I'm sorry to wake you, Miss Robertson, but I need to check your vitals. I'll be as quick as I can, then I'll leave you alone to rest. My name is Julie, by the way, and if you need anything through the night, don't hesitate to use your buzzer."

"Um, Julie, do you think I could have a wash and move position? It feels so warm in here, and I can't seem to get comfortable," I told her as I tried to alter my position.

"Of course, Miss Robertson. I'll just finish getting your stats together, then I'll sit you up and bring a bowl of water."

"Could I go to a bathroom instead, please?" I asked, but she shook her head.

"I'm afraid the surgeon said bed rest for twenty-four hours, but he'll be back to review you in the morning. You have a catheter fitted, so you don't have to get up and use the toilet, and I can bring you a bedpan if you need one."

"No, it's not that," I quickly replied, trying to hide my

embarrassment from Kolya. "I just want to feel clean. And I haven't got any soap or anything with me."

"I asked the spa staff at my hotel to put together a few essentials for you, *malyutka*, and my assistant organised some nightwear and other items of clothing to be delivered earlier this evening. Unfortunately, we were unable to find your shoe size from the ones you wore, so the ladies at the spa sent their usual towelling slippers." Kolya gestured towards some bags next to the wall. "We didn't want to disturb you while you were sleeping, so we left the clothes in the bags."

I glanced over and spotted the name on six of the bags. Harvey Nichols. Looking back at Kolya, I shook my head.

"I appreciate you getting me some clothing, but honestly, I don't have any money to pay you for them. I can understand you paying for private healthcare, but buying me clothes from Harvey Nichols is way too over the top. So I'm sorry if it's messing you and your assistant around, but I just can't accept them, Kolya."

"Nonsense, *malyutka*. This small amount of clothing is nothing to me. You can and will accept them. You needed clothes, and now you have some. They had to cut away the clothing from your upper body when you were brought in, and there was blood on your other clothes, so they were disposed of. Now, if you wish, I can help you with your bathing, or I can leave the room while the nurse helps you," Kolya stated as he brought over the biggest wash bag I had ever seen.

I could tell from the look in his eyes that his offer was sincere. That he would help me wash if I wanted. But I shook my head and told him I'd be happier if the nurse did it.

"Very well, *malyutka*. I will go for a coffee and wait until you are decent. Lucas, my driver, and another guard are right outside if you need anything while I am gone," Kolya informed me while heading towards the door.

He turned to face me as he closed the door behind him, and I saw so much concern in his eyes. It kind of threw me, to be honest, and I didn't know how to deal with it. After all, there had been few people in my life who'd shown any real concern or regard for my welfare in the past. So, I gave Kolya a wary smile and watched as he closed the door.

Nurse Julie went over to a doorway that was hidden behind a screen. It was then I realised the room I was in had an en-suite bathroom. I heard her opening and closing cupboard doors, then turning on taps. Moments later, she came out of the bathroom with a bowl filled with warm water.

I unzipped the wash bag and carefully took out its contents. There was face wash, shower cream, a face cloth, toner, moisturiser, and eye cream, all by Elemis. Next came Philip Kingsley shampoo and conditioner, along with a brush and comb. I knew they were expensive brands. I'd seen them when Jean took Sarah and me out window shopping in Leeds.

Julie smiled and said, "Let's remove this hospital gown first, then I'll leave you to wash where you can while I look in the bags for a nighty or pyjamas. After you've washed and dressed, I'll bring you a cup of Horlicks or hot chocolate, and later, if you've kept it all down, I'll request some food from the restaurant. How does that sound?"

It all sounded good—until she began removing my gown. Pain hit me hard, but I pushed through it somehow, and after Julie had pumped a bit of the face wash onto the wet cloth, I began to clean my face, neck, and upper body. Although doing this was exhausting, I immediately felt the benefit, and my mood lifted. A fresh bowl of water later and I was able to clean the rest of my body. Julie helped me wash my back, legs, and feet.

Although I'd tried to keep as clean as I could while living on the streets, it's just not the same when you're strip washing over a sink in the disabled toilets at McDonald's.

I was so grateful to feel fresher than before. Julie took a roll-on deodorant, toothbrush and toothpaste out of the wash bag, and after bringing me two cups of water, I began to brush my teeth. She looked through yet another bag and brought a button-down satin nightshirt over to the bed. After removing the tags and the IV tubes for a moment, she helped me put it on. It looked expensive and felt so soft against my skin.

Julie took the water into the bathroom and came back with a mirror. My shoulder-length, copper-coloured curly hair was untamed and frizzy, but without shampooing and conditioning it, there really wasn't anything I could do.

Julie suggested mixing a small amount of conditioner with water and running that through it, and as there was nothing else to be done, I reluctantly agreed. Surprisingly, it did help a little, and at least it stopped me looking like I'd stuck my fingers into a live plug socket. Why I even cared about my appearance so much while still in pain, I really couldn't say. I think mind over matter had a lot to do with it. Kind of *'if I look better, I will feel better,'* and for the most part, I felt that it was working.

Looking once more in the mirror, I couldn't help but notice how pale my lips were. Usually, they were a dusky rose colour, but whether it was due to pain or blood loss, for the moment they matched my pale skin. I looked tired, and even the freckles across my nose and cheeks had less colour. My amber eyes looked slightly bloodshot and held no sparkle. *This is what being shot does for you,* I thought to myself, and I laughed a little despite the seriousness of the situation.

Julie looked at me like I'd grown another head, which made me laugh even harder. Without warning, the laughter suddenly turned to tears, and try as I might, I couldn't seem to stop. Julie tried to soothe me, but it didn't help.

I didn't hear the door opening, but I recognised the familiar manly scent of Kolya when he kissed the top of my head and then rested his forehead against mine. Taking hold of both my hands, he sat on the edge of the bed and began saying something in what I assumed to be Russian. I couldn't understand it, of course, but I listened to the words all the same, and pretty soon, my sobs began to subside. Kolya kissed my fingers again before letting go of my hands and grabbing some tissues from a box by the side of my bed. I took them gratefully, wiping the tears from my eyes before blowing my nose.

"I'm sorry," I murmured, not quite meeting his eyes. "I'm not usually a crier. I don't know what came over me."

"Hush, *malyutka*. The last twenty-four hours have been

very traumatic for you. In fact, the last few years of your life have been very traumatic, from what you have told me. It is understandable you broke down for a moment. And often it is good to do that. It's how we let things go and move on. If we keep these emotions locked away, eventually, we break, and that is much harder to fix. So cry all you want when you need to, little one. There will be no judgement from me or mine when you do."

I glanced up at his beautifully sculpted features. Once again, his eyes expressed genuine care and concern, and I became lost in their depths. Something hit me deep in my chest; a sensation so strong it took my breath away. It was an odd feeling… as though something was pulling me towards him while sinking low into my belly at the same time. But it didn't cause me any physical pain, just a strong feeling of having butterflies. I couldn't seem to tear my gaze away from him and stayed that way until his hand cupped the side of my face. I leaned into it and closed my eyes, enjoying the feeling of his thumb as it skimmed my cheek with a featherlight touch.

I couldn't understand my reaction to Kolya. I'd known very few men personally, choosing to avoid them whenever I could. Seeing all the different men my mother earned her money from probably hadn't helped. I had never known a father, grandfather, uncle or any other male family member, and I didn't get on with any of the male social workers at The Willows.

Kolya seemed different. I sensed he wouldn't ever give me cause to doubt his intentions towards me, and even though I'd only known him a matter of hours, I felt he was someone I could rely on. Of course, the warm, fuzzy feelings I was having towards this virtual stranger could be completely wrong. A side effect of the medication, perhaps?

I pushed those thoughts aside for the moment and just enjoyed the feeling of being cared for, and as Kolya continued to stroke my cheek, I fell into a long and peaceful sleep.

9

KOLYA

How long had I sat on the edge of her bed, stroking her cheek? I truly did not know. Time escaped me as I watched her eyes close when she drifted off to sleep.

I knew she was sleeping deeply, leaving no need for my soothing touch.

Yet I could not seem to stop.

Touching her was as essential to me as breathing in those few peaceful moments.

I carried on for a little while longer, marvelling at the softness of her skin. Her vibrant, coppery-red hair with its wayward curls stood out in stark contrast against the paleness of her complexion. Tess was a true beauty, naturally so.

Her youth was obvious while she lay sleeping; only when her eyes were open did she seem older. Not that she had any of the lines that appear with age, but in those dark-amber orbs, you could almost see all the stress, pain, and poverty that had been her life so far.

My poor Tess. I could not believe what I was hearing when she told me about her past. The story of a child born to a drug addict with no other family to care for her. Of how she was attacked by the man who was beating her mother. How she was placed into foster care with a genuine, caring woman, only to be taken away when fate intervened. If that wasn't enough, she was also being hunted by despicable men who target underage girls. The fact she was recovering in a hospital bed could have made her vulnerable to those men.

I wondered, at that moment, if Tess realised how her life was about to change. She now had me to keep her safe. My protection, my wealth, my everything. If this young woman ever needed anything, I would see it taken care of. There wasn't anything I would not do for her. I would move mountains, pull stars from the night sky, and give her the whole world, for she deserved all of that and so much more.

After brushing my fingertips over her cheek one last time, I moved my hand away from her face, steadily getting up from my seat on the bed beside her.

I suddenly felt bereft, like I'd lost something precious—something I needed desperately. I looked around the room as though it could provide the answer to why I felt this way, but it gave me nothing.

Before I took my seat by the side of the bed, I bent low to place a chaste kiss on Tess's cheek.

And that's when it hit me.

An intense feeling of rightness enveloped me as my lips

made contact where my fingertips had been moments earlier. I felt whole. Happy. Strong. Like I could rule the world just by being in her presence. I kept my lips in contact with her skin a few seconds longer, breathing her in, storing the scent of her in my memory.

When I finally pulled away, Tess moved her tongue over her lips before pressing them together and then sighing. She was still asleep, unaware of the life-altering moment I had just experienced. I stared down at her, unable to tear my gaze away. I knew then that Tess had not just given me my future—she would be a part of it, too. But what role she would play in my life, I did not yet know.

10

TESS

I awoke to a splashing sound that was coming from the en-suite bathroom. I carefully manoeuvred myself, so I could see through the open door. Kolya stood shirtless in front of the sink as he washed his face, wearing only a pair of grey trousers.

Seeing the muscles in his tattooed back flex as he moved mesmerised me. I couldn't tear my gaze away. When he was done, he turned to retrieve something that was hanging on the back of the open door. I watched while he put on a pale-blue shirt, noting that he also had a tattoo on his left shoulder, yet none on his muscular chest and abs. I wondered what significance the body art held for him.

"Good morning, Tess. How long have you been awake?" he asked, smiling as he walked towards me.

"Not long; a few minutes at the most."

"What would you like for breakfast? An orderly came by

with a menu about an hour ago. I thought I'd wait until you were awake so we could eat together."

He passed the menu along to me, and I was surprised by the choice. As I read through the cooked breakfast options, my stomach began to growl, and I realised I'd not eaten anything since yesterday morning. I chose a grilled full English breakfast with poached eggs, and Kolya did the same.

"I'm due in a meeting at eleven, but it's not too far from here, so I can stay until ten thirty. The doctor will be here before ten, so we'll find out how long you'll need to stay in the hospital. I have business in the capital today and tomorrow, so I'll send Franco or Nate to sit with you. There have been no sightings of the men who were following you, but I'm not willing to take any chances. They followed you all the way to London, so I do not think they will give up so easily. As soon as you are well enough to leave, we will make the journey to my home in Oxford. We can go by helicopter rather than have you sit uncomfortably in a car for an hour and forty minutes."

"Helicopter?" I questioned nervously.

"Yes, it will be much quicker. Barely half an hour, in fact. Getting in and out of London by car is so tedious and time-consuming because of all the traffic. I always prefer to travel by helicopter wherever possible."

I didn't know what to say to him. I was grateful to him for caring about my physical comfort. But a helicopter? And he said he was taking me to his home. I must have looked a little confused because he explained further what would be happening.

"It is my understanding, from what you have said, that you are homeless, have no family, and have been living on the streets. Obviously, that is unacceptable, and as I told you yesterday, you saved my life, so I will make sure I give you a good life in return. That starts with a home and food in your belly. You can continue with your education, and I will see that you are financially secure. I also want to make sure you are kept safe, and the best way to do that is for you to stay with me. As you are aware, I always have my close protection team with me. Apart from that incident yesterday."

Kolya took my hand in his and kissed my fingers once again. Looking into my eyes, he said, "I wish you hadn't been hurt, *malyutka*, but you saved me, so now your life is bound to mine. I will see you thrive and become strong, happy, and successful. If there is anything you need, you will have it without question."

A knock at the door interrupted Kolya as he was about to say something else, so instead, he went to the door and held it open, allowing the porter to wheel in our breakfasts.

A short time after our breakfast plates were taken away, two doctors and a nurse came into my room. A tall man with salt-and-pepper hair introduced himself as Mr Grayson, and his colleague, a beautiful Indian lady, was Dr Rath.

I found out that Mr Grayson was the surgeon who'd removed the bullet from below my collarbone. He said I was lucky. As it was on my left side, if it had been a few inches lower, it could have caused irreparable damage to my heart. He explained details about where the bullet entered and said he'd had no difficulty removing it. He assured me there was no significant nerve damage but told me I'd be quite sore for some time.

Mr Grayson said that due to the amount of blood loss and my previous injuries, he would be happier if I stayed in the hospital another night. He recommended physiotherapy to aid movement and offered to help set up some private sessions at Kolya's home. It was clear he and Kolya were friends, and I tried not to laugh when they began verbally sparring about winning their next game of squash. When Mr Grayson got up to leave, Kolya followed him out of the door, telling me he would be a few moments and that Ivan and Nate were outside the door on guard duty if I needed them.

Dr Rath asked me questions about my pain, telling me to lift my arm in certain ways to see how my movement was affected. She advised me I'd be getting a sling to support my arm during the day, which should lessen the pain and avoid further strain on the wound site. She also said because my stats were looking much better, she'd get my catheter removed so I'd be able to get up and move around.

She enquired whether I'd ever been anaemic. I shook my head and said I hadn't, as far as I was aware. Dr Rath then asked if I had heavy periods, and I had to admit I did. She advised me that my blood count had been very low, even considering the blood loss from being shot, so they'd given me a transfusion during surgery. She told me they'd like to repeat my blood tests and would give me a course of iron tablets if needed. Dr Rath also asked if I'd like to discuss starting on a contraceptive pill—to regulate my periods and make them less heavy. She said she'd be more than happy to talk to me about it before I left.

Kolya came back into the room, so once again, I shook my head, saying nothing. I didn't want to talk about periods, contraceptives, or anything of that nature in front of a man.

He stood at the end of my bed and stared at me.

He seemed tense, and for a time bore no movement apart from his heavy breathing. I didn't ask what was wrong; I wasn't sure I wanted to know. But something told me it had a lot to do with what he and Mr Grayson had discussed after they'd left the room. No doubt confidentiality about medical records and past admissions went out of the window when someone was paying for hospital treatment at one of the best private hospitals in the country.

I shivered, feeling exposed and vulnerable. But while I was recovering, there was very little I could do about it. I'd told Kolya what had happened to me when I was attacked by Philip Casey, but if he'd had it explained by a doctor or seen it in writing, I suppose it would sound much worse than it did when I skirted around the story.

"Do not fear me, *malyutka*. As I told you before, I will never hurt you," Kolya stated while walking towards me. Dr Rath, who was still busy marking something off my hospital chart, looked up at Kolya as he spoke.

"Dr Rath, may I have a word with Tess for a moment? I have to leave for a meeting shortly, and I will be gone most of the day," he said rather abruptly.

"Tess?" Doctor Rath questioned. Kolya's commanding presence did not phase Dr Rath at all. Her petite stature seemed to grow a little when she sensed my apprehension.

"It's okay, Dr Rath, thank you." I glanced her way and smiled, hoping to ease any concerns she had about my welfare. She picked up the rest of my charts and, with one last look back at Kolya, left the room.

Dr Rath's actions empowered me. Looking Kolya in the eye, I told him, "Go on, then. Get it over with. Something you've been told has pissed you off, so spit it out, Mr Barinov, instead of growling at the staff."

He seemed taken aback, either by my words or the fact I'd called him by his surname. I'd certainly shocked him, but he didn't seem angry. He just looked sad. Now anger, I could have taken; I was used to seeing that. But Kolya looked like he just felt sorry for me. I couldn't accept that, so I turned my head as much as I could without causing myself any pain and whispered, "Just leave me alone. Please."

He hesitated for a moment, and I thought he'd do as I asked. Instead, he sat on the edge of the bed and lifted my right hand, kissing each of my fingertips. It was something he'd done before, but this time his kisses lingered on each finger. Then he took my hand and pressed it against his cheek.

"Don't be upset with me, little one. I know you told me all about yourself and what happened to you, but to see it all in writing came as quite a shock. My anger is not with you, although you held much back, it seems. I am angry with the man who hurt you, even though he is dead, and I'm angry that you were ever in that situation in the first place. I'm also saddened beyond belief that you are in pain after risking your life to save mine. I wish I could trade places with you right now to take your pain away." He leaned forward and whispered softly in my ear, "I will give you the world."

His breath was hot against my cheek as he pulled away, and I turned to look at him. Our faces were so close that when he leaned towards me once again, I thought he was going to kiss my lips, so I held my breath and closed my eyes. Instead, he pressed his forehead to mine, saying, "I don't want to leave you, but I have to go."

Kolya got up from the bed, and I wasn't sure whether I felt relieved or disappointed. A heated blush crept up my neck and cheeks, and I didn't dare meet his eyes.

I heard him gather his things together and watched him open the door. Kolya turned to say goodbye, and I gave him a small wave as he left. When the door closed, I let out a huge sigh.

What the hell was wrong with me? Why did I think such a gorgeous, sophisticated, wealthy guy would want to kiss me? And why would I want him to?

I'd sworn off the opposite sex with ease. I mean, if the men my mum brought home weren't enough to put me off, the lads at school definitely had. I hadn't had a boyfriend since I was in junior school, and I didn't think holding hands with Craig Smith during assembly counted as having a real boyfriend.

Sarah used to wind me up about not going out with anyone, and I used to say that if Johnny Depp were to come along, I would date him in a flash. Sadly, Johnny never came to visit me, so I remained single. But imagining someone like Kolya Barinov wanting to kiss me was ludicrous. A homeless, inexperienced seventeen-year-old. What a catch I was. Not!

Kolya was probably just doing his bit for the poor when he was being nice to me—or trying to appease his misplaced guilt that I'd been shot instead of him.

I decided to put thoughts of my first kiss out of my mind until Johnny Depp came calling. After all, I figured there was as much chance of that as being kissed on the lips by Kolya. It did feel nice when he kissed me on the fingers, though. I wondered why he did that. Was it a Russian thing?

My thoughts were interrupted when Maria, the nurse from yesterday, came in to remove my catheter.

11

TESS

Nate stayed with me the rest of the morning. I felt comfortable with him. He was smart and funny, and we'd played checkers for an hour or so. I told him we called it draughts here in England, but he said that sounded lame. He brought me several fashion magazines, a balloon, and a teddy with *get well soon* embroidered on it. His kindness touched me, and I told him how much it meant to me. Nate said I was one of them now, so I should get used to it.

Nurse Maria came by about an hour after lunch and asked if I wanted to have a bath or a shower. I was desperate to soak in a warm bath but needed help washing my hair. I wasn't happy having someone seeing me naked; when I was in hospital before, I'd hated it. But I wanted to feel clean, and I couldn't do it myself.

Nurse Maria was very thorough when washing and conditioning my unruly hair. She had a similar hair type, so she knew how hard it was to tame.

Once I was out of the bath, Dr Rath came to examine my wound and put a clean, dry dressing over it. By this time, I was in a lot of pain. All the day's activity had been exhausting, and strong pain medication left me drowsier still.

Nate came back and sat quietly beside my bed, reading one of the magazines he'd bought me, while I fell into a deep and restful sleep.

When I awoke, Nate had gone, and in his place was an extremely tall hulk of a man who introduced himself as Ivan. He had a strong Russian accent and seemed to be a man of few words.

"Hello, I am Ivan. You want to eat?" were the words he greeted me with. Due to his sheer muscular bulk and furious look on his face, I wasn't sure what to make of him. But I recalled the words Kolya had said—that I had nothing to fear from him or his staff—so I tried my best to be extra friendly.

I held out my hand to him, saying, "Hello, Ivan, I'm Tess, and I'm very pleased to meet you. Kolya said you've been guarding my door. Thank you for that."

Ivan stared at me for what seemed like minutes, and I wondered if he hadn't understood what I'd said, given the strength of his accent. But just as I was about to drop my hand, he leaned forward in the chair and took my hand in his, giving me such a vigorous handshake I flinched a little in pain. Ivan stood and apologised, a bright red blush spreading quickly over his pale face and neck. I assured him I was fine, but I could tell he didn't quite believe me.

Trying to make conversation, I asked him if he came from the same part of Russia as Kolya. Ivan pointed his index finger back at himself and said in a proud voice, "I am his cousin."

I smiled at him, and he smiled back, nodding his head. He didn't look much like Kolya, apart from the fact he had the same brown hair, but he must have stood at least seven inches taller. I'd seen Kolya's muscular chest and back this morning, yet I could tell through his clothing that Ivan was bigger—like a professional bodybuilder. That, combined with his height, would scare the shit out of most people. His eyes weren't as pale blue as Kolya's, but when he smiled, they sparkled a little, making him look kind of handsome and semi-friendly. Still intimidating as hell, though.

When a hospital orderly came by and brought me a menu, I asked Ivan if he would stay and have dinner with me. He seemed thrilled I had asked and quickly took the menu the orderly offered him. I ordered hunter's chicken with new potatoes, green beans and carrots, along with ice cream for dessert. Ivan ordered soup and a roll to start with, then he doubled the size of the hunter's chicken dinner I had ordered, with a side of garlic bread. He also ordered ice cream and apple pie for dessert.

With Ivan being a big guy, I knew he'd need plenty of food, but when it came, he devoured everything he'd ordered while I was still eating my main meal. The worrying thing was, he still looked hungry, so I gave him my ice cream and asked the orderly—who came to take away our plates—if we could have some tea and biscuits.

I could get used to private health care. For the food choices alone, it was amazing.

Ivan and I began to relax in each other's company, and when they brought in our tea and biscuits, Ivan got up to pour.

I stifled a laugh at the delicate way he handled the tiny bone china cup and saucer, but he didn't seem to notice. When I told him I didn't take sugar in my tea, I thought he would faint with shock. It wasn't until I saw him put four sugars in his tiny cup that I found out why. Apparently, Ivan had a very sweet tooth. I handed him the plate with the biscuits and told him to take them all. He hesitated a little, then looked at me suspiciously.

"Why do you not eat?" he asked, leaning towards me. "Do you have pain? Feel sick?"

I shook my head. "No, I just feel full."

"You need to eat. You will not heal if you do not eat. Do you not like this food?" he asked.

Without waiting for my reply, he walked towards the door.

I told him I was fine and definitely not hungry, but Ivan ignored me and said something to another guard who was outside my door.

He came to sit beside me again and poured us both another tea before declaring, "Tess, you will not worry. Ivan can fix this."

We sat back in comfortable silence while I racked my brain to find something to talk about. I thought about what Kolya had said about travelling to his home in a helicopter, so

I asked Ivan if he'd ever travelled in one. His laugh was deep, almost booming throughout the room, and I wondered what was so funny.

"I fly helicopter as well as guard, so yes, *milaya moya,* I have travelled in many. Are you nervous about flying?"

"Yes. I haven't been in a helicopter or an aeroplane before. Maybe I would be better off making the journey to Kolya's home by car. He said I'd be more comfortable if we went by helicopter, but I won't be comfortable if I end up with travel sickness," I stated.

"Are you travel-sick before?" he asked. His English phrasing was slightly off, but his concern was genuine.

"I haven't travelled much, so I wouldn't really know. I went to Leeds once on the train with my foster mother, and I was fine. I came to London on the train and was okay then, too. I once went on a coach to the seaside on a school trip, and I can't remember being sick then, but I was only about seven, so who knows what I would be like now."

"You will be good, *milaya moya*. Trust Ivan on this," he declared, winking at me.

"What does *milaya moya* mean?" I asked, changing the subject.

"My sweet," he answered shyly.

"You would be the sweet one, Ivan. You take way too much sugar in your tea."

His laugh boomed out through the room again, and he slapped his hand against his thigh.

A short time later, there was a knock at the door, and then in walked a guard with three huge Domino's pizza boxes.

"Hello, I'm Jonesy," he announced, placing the pizzas beside me on the wheeled table.

"Ivan said you were still hungry, so I ordered four pizzas and some sides. I'm going to grab a few slices, then I'll be out of your way."

Jonesy took out five slices and slapped them onto a lid he'd torn from a box. He took a huge bite out of one of them and gave me a wink before walking out of the door. Ivan handed me a pizza, onto which he tipped some potato wedges before commanding me to "Eat!"

I really didn't want to eat anything else, but I didn't want to seem ungrateful either, so I ate a slice of pizza, some wedges, and a chocolate brownie. I was now uncomfortably full but happy.

I couldn't believe only two days ago I was begging for money to buy food. Now I was being ordered to eat by a Russian *Mr Universe,* who was currently devouring his second pizza. It was like the last few days had been a strange dream, though if it was a dream, I really didn't want to wake up.

12

TESS

Just after a nurse came in with my medication, Kolya arrived at the door carrying a medium-sized paper bag. He greeted Ivan, and then placed the bag at the end of my bed.

"Good evening, Tess. You are looking much better. How do you feel?" he asked.

"I'm okay," I answered truthfully. The pain had eased a little, although it still hurt like hell. The medication they gave me was doing its job. Last night, not so much.

Kolya scanned the room, noting the pizza boxes and cans of soft drinks Ivan had procured. He cast his gaze over to his cousin and shook his head.

"Ivan, Tess should be eating healthy food to aid her recovery, not this takeaway rubbish," Kolya voiced harshly. I felt bad for Ivan. His intentions were good, and I didn't want him to get into trouble.

"I'm sorry, Kolya, it was my fault. I didn't fancy anything

on the menu, and I haven't had pizza in such a long time. Ivan said he'd send out for some if I'd eat it." Both Ivan and Kolya stared straight at me.

Ivan huffed out, "She eats like a *myshka*. I had to make sure she was well-fed."

"Well, you can take these boxes away; it looks like you've been having a party in here." With his tone, he was trying for stern, but Kolya's slight grin gave away the fact that he wasn't angry. He bent forward and kissed me on the top of my head before whispering in my ear, "You didn't have to lie for him. We all know that Ivan is a pizza addict."

"As well as sugar," I answered. Then I looked at Ivan and said, *"Milaya moya."*

He came towards me, blue eyes sparkling, saying, "As I am male, how you say the words is different. You need to say *miliy moy.* Try it."

"*Miliy moy* Ivan."

"Very good, Tess. You can also say *moy sladkiy.* We will have her speaking Russian very soon, cousin," Ivan told Kolya, slapping him on the back before leaving with his pizza boxes.

"I see you and Ivan have made friends," muttered Kolya, arching his back, no doubt feeling the ache from the slap that Ivan left there.

"I thought he was a bit scary at first, but he's actually a big softie," I told him.

"Tell that to my back," Kolya replied, taking off his jacket. "The man doesn't know his own strength."

"He said you and he are cousins," I told him.

"My mother and his mother were sisters. Ivan is six years younger than me. Our mothers passed away within ten months of each other. Both had breast cancer. Our grandmother died from it too, but that was many years before my mother. Of course, there is much more to be done nowadays with modern medicine, but my mother died twenty-four years ago when treatments were limited, although it seems like only yesterday."

"I'm sorry to hear that, Kolya. How old were you at the time?"

"I had just turned sixteen, so Ivan was around ten when my aunt died. It was all too much for our grandfather to bear; he had a fatal heart attack not long after my mother's funeral. It was a terrible time for my family. I have given much towards research for a cure for this awful disease, and lately, it seems there is more hope to be had."

"Maybe she's in heaven looking down on you?" I told him, wanting to give him some comfort. "My foster mum used to say that those who've gone before look down on us from heaven and guide us on our way."

"I used to think that, too. But then Catherine had her riding accident, and yet again, there was a husband without his wife, another son without his mother. She wouldn't have let that happen. She was fiercely protective of her sons, no matter how big we grew."

"Maybe she sent me to save you," I suggested.

"Maybe," he said, a hint of a smile appearing on his face, replacing the faraway look he'd had for the last few minutes.

"Of course, my mother wasn't looking out for me, or she wouldn't have let me get shot," I stated.

"Tess, your mother may have sent you to me to help you just the same."

"That's a messed-up way of looking at it. Although, thinking about my mum, messed up would be just about right."

Even I could hear the hurt in my words.

"Look at me, *malyutka.* Your life with your mother wasn't good, I get that. But when it came down to it, she tried to save you. She took that man's life to stop him hurting you. So she may have sent you to me in order to stop these men from getting to you. You just got hurt in the process."

Thinking about it further, I conceded that Kolya could be right. I'd discussed it as some sort of divine intervention with Nate earlier. I knew no matter how I'd ended up in Kolya's path, he was going to help keep me safe from Tariq, Farid, and Hassan. And that seemed like heaven to me.

Kolya took the bag from the bottom of the bed and brought it to me, then he reached inside and took out a box with a mobile phone on the front. It was a brand-new smartphone and appeared quite complicated to use. Kolya handed it to me.

"It's fully set up with a new SIM card inside, and all the numbers you'll need are already on there, Tess. So if you need to contact me, day or night, just call or text me."

He got out some paperwork and a small instruction manual. "It's an Android phone, so you need a Gmail account. I've already set one up for you, and the email address and password for it is right here. I wouldn't recommend using your own email address, if you have one, in case anyone tries to trace you through it."

"Is this for me?" I asked while I carefully handled the phone.

"Of course," he replied. "I've included a plain white case, although you can choose another if you wish, and there are also headphones, but I would rather you not wear them here. It is best to be aware of your surroundings in case one of the guards needs to move you quickly," Kolya warned, and I got the feeling he was keeping something from me.

I waited for him to say what that was, but he didn't.

Kolya took the phone out of my hands and quickly snapped a photo of me before handing it back.

"The camera is exceptionally good on this model," he said.

I looked at the photo and groaned.

"I look awful in that pic," I told him while trying to work out how to delete it. My hair, although much tamer after my bath, had gone quite frizzy again after I'd slept.

"You look lovely, *malyutka*," he said with a smile. "I had a surprise for you today, but something has come up that needs my attention, so you will see your surprise tomorrow. Unfortunately, I don't think I'll be back to stay with you tonight, so I'll send in one of my guards to sit with you if you wish."

I tried to hide my disappointment as Kolya grabbed his jacket from the chair.

"I don't need you to send a guard in to sit with me. I think I might sleep better without anyone here," I told him, hoping he would listen. Nate and Ivan were lovely guys, but I didn't think it was right to make them babysit me all night.

"There will be two guards here anyway if you need them. I'm hopeful after speaking with your doctor that you will be able to come home with me tomorrow. As long as you can control your pain and you haven't developed an infection, we could leave around lunchtime. Now, I must say goodbye and goodnight, Tess. Remember, if you need to call me, you have my number on your phone."

Something was niggling at me about his abrupt manner. When Kolya leaned over and kissed me on my cheek, I asked him what was wrong. He sat down again and sighed, then looked at me for a moment before speaking.

"One of the men from the photographs on your friend's phone, Farid Ali, came to my hotel. We had left the phone switched on, and I was right: they were tracing it. Not long after we apprehended him, another man we believe to be Tariq Akbar was spotted near the entrance of the hospital. Unfortunately, we were unable to capture this man."

A chilling wave of nausea swept over me. I was at a distinct disadvantage being laid up in a hospital bed, and I couldn't wait to leave.

"Can't I go home with you tonight?" I asked. He shook his head and lifted my hand to his mouth, kissing my fingertips again.

"Please do not be frightened, *malyutka*. You are well protected here. I am going to question this Farid and try to find out where your friend is, and what he wants with you. Although, from what you have told me, I can already guess."

"What are you going to do with him after you've questioned him? Are you going to call the police and show them the phone?" I asked.

"I will take care of it for you, *malyutka*. That is all you need to know right now."

Kolya's expression became tense. He looked away from me for a few moments before adding, "I vowed to keep you safe, Tess. No matter what that entails, I have to make it so."

I nodded my head and then thanked him for the phone. Looking back at me, his tense expression lifted into a smile. He stood up, ready to leave, and a frisson of fear coursed through me. Tariq had been near the hospital. What if he came back again?

"Under the circumstances, I suppose it would be better if a guard stayed in the room with me. I mean, sleeping in that big, comfy chair would be better than hanging around in the hallway," I conceded, trying to hide my anxiousness.

"As you wish," replied Kolya as he turned to leave. "But they certainly won't be sleeping, Tess, so you do not need to worry."

All the same, I knew I would miss Kolya's presence. So, before he closed the door, I called out to him. As he stepped back into the room, I took a photo of him using my new phone. He was startled at first, but then he laughed, so I took another before he left.

13

KOLYA

Walking away from Tess while she still looked so scared was one of the hardest things I'd ever done. But I couldn't stay tonight; the threat to Tess's life had to be handled immediately.

I needed to question Farid Ali, even though I'd like nothing more than to tear him apart with my bare hands as soon as I saw him. Tess was worried about her friend, but I had a feeling she was no longer alive.

Sarah knew too much. Had seen too much. She was just fifteen years old.

A child.

These men were nothing more than paedophiles. They deliberately used the girl's vulnerability to their advantage. It made me feel sick to my stomach to think of what she may have gone through.

Lucas opened the car door as we got to it, his expression as dark as my own. Jonesy was already in the driver's seat.

"We need to wait for Ivan, boss. He's making one last tour of the grounds before we leave. He's worried that this Tariq fella will come back tonight, and he wanted to stay just in case," Jonesy informed me.

"I have four guards at the hospital tonight: one at each entrance and two outside her room. Tess will be safe. He must not doubt that." In a way, I said it to reassure myself as much as Jonesy.

"I know that, boss. But it seems he's taken quite a shine to her. Said he's got her speaking Russian."

I knew my cousin had warmed to Tess when I'd entered the room. But what did Jonesy mean by *"taken quite a shine to her"*?

Ivan wasn't normally an easy person to get to know. He could be quite gruff and reserved. His height and muscle mass often made people wary of him, and he played on that a little. But it appeared he and Tess were friendly and comfortable with each other. I admit to feeling a slight pang of jealousy when she'd called him *my sweet*. Obviously, he must have called Tess that for her to try to say it back to him.

I tilted my head back and ran my hand over my face, trying to clear my thoughts. I should not be so worried about what was simply a well-used term of endearment. Why it bothered me at all was something I couldn't get my head around.

Before I could ponder the reason behind it, Ivan opened the door and came to sit in the back of the car beside me.

"I know you have one of them back at the hotel," he said

gruffly as we pulled out of the carpark into the heavy London traffic.

"Yes, Franco has him in a room that's ready for refurbishing. I need to obtain information from him, then we'll get him out of the hotel as soon as possible."

"You would let him go? The man who came to find Tess and did unspeakable things to her friend? Kolya, tell me this cannot be so?"

Ivan had asked me those questions in Russian, his voice raised in disbelief and anger. So I answered him back in Russian, my tone cold and determined.

"I did not say he'd be breathing when he left."

14

KOLYA

Sitting across the room from Farid Ali without having caused him physical pain was an arduous task. Franco stood to my left near the door, his intense stare fixed on the wretched man's face.

Plastic sheeting covered the carpeted floor beneath the chair upon which Farid sat. Cable ties secured his arms and legs so he couldn't move from his current position. Franco had stripped him down to his boxer shorts, the contents of his pockets placed on the lamp table beside me. The area around his right eye was swollen, and his lower lip split. Seeing the injuries Franco inflicted did not calm the raging beast inside me—the one that demanded I tear out his beating heart. But I needed to keep control in order to gain the information I required to find Tess's friend.

I took a deep breath before I spoke, keeping my tone even

and unemotional, detached from the scene the carefully staged room created.

"You have been searching for someone here in London. Someone under my protection. Why?"

"I don't know what you're talking about. I don't even know who you are!"

Although he was anxious, I noted a hint of defiance in his voice. Confidence, even. As if he thought this whole setup was just a threat. The man was a fool.

"You were searching for a young woman named Tess Robertson. I believe you are extremely well acquainted with her friend, Sarah Crowther. Tell me, Mr Ali, what were your plans for Tess had you found her? And where have you taken Sarah?"

"I don't know what the fuck you're talking about. I don't know anyone called Sarah or Tess."

"I would advise you against lying, Mr Ali. It is not something I tolerate."

Franco took two steps towards Farid, making a fist with his right hand and raising it slightly, his footsteps creating a crinkling sound on the plastic sheeting.

"What are you doing? I'm not lying. I don't know these girls. No, stop—"

I nodded my head just once, then watched with barely disguised satisfaction as Franco slammed his fist into Farid's cheekbone. The audible crack indicated a possible fracture—the howling cry and subsequent dazed look confirmed the hoped-for diagnosis. Franco glanced my way, a sinister grin replacing his usual stern look. Another nod from me, and he reclaimed his position beside the door, arms folded, his eyes fixed on the whimpering male.

"Now, let's try this again, shall we? Why were you—along with Tariq and Hassan Akbar—searching for Tess Robertson?"

Farid remained silent, apart from the occasional moan or whimper. His left eye was swelling fast, and I watched with morbid fascination as it closed completely after less than a minute. His right eye looked glassy; the unmistakable sheen of tears evident to all. Did he think they would garner him sympathy from me? If he did, he was very much mistaken.

I nodded again at Franco, making sure Farid had noticed me do so. Franco barely moved this time before Farid answered. His words were what I'd expected to hear when I first entered the room.

"They know where I am, you know. They'll have tracked my phone via GPS by now. I bet they're waiting outside this hotel for me."

I held my hand up to halt Franco's movements, then signalled for him to stand down.

"I hope you are right, Mr Ali. My guards would like nothing more than to apprehend your friends as soon as possible. I have them stationed at various points around the hotel, and there are several at the hospital where Tariq Akbar was recently spotted," I told him.

Farid's right eye flicked from me to Franco, then back again. His chest rose and fell in quick succession, the earlier confidence he'd displayed now lost amongst the hopelessness of the situation he found himself in. I wondered what words he would use next to try and gain his freedom.

"When I don't check in with them, they'll know something happened and will send the police. They'll trace my phone and see me entering this hotel on CCTV."

"That's what I'm planning on," I told him smugly. I removed my jacket and tie, making myself more comfortable.

"You see, Mr Farid Ali, aged thirty, from Doncaster, South Yorkshire, I know all about you and your colleagues." I took out my phone and brought up the email I'd received earlier from Kevin. "You are married to Shazia, have an eight-year-old son named Sajid, and a two-year-old daughter named after your mother, Rabia. Tell me, Mr Ali, how would the women in your life feel about you treating the young girls you targeted the way you did? How would you feel if your family were treated the same way?"

"The women in my family are nothing like those girls," he declared angrily. "Females in our culture have respect for themselves and those around them. Good Muslim women. Those girls deserved everything they got, plain and simple. They dress like common whores—with their short skirts and tops that show more of their tits than they cover. They go out like that day and night, flaunting themselves. It's like they're begging to get fucked."

I noticed Franco's body stiffen, and he again made his hand into a fist, though he did not move to strike the bastard who'd tried justifying his actions.

"The girls you targeted were vulnerable children. They were likely desperate for attention from someone—anyone they thought would care for them, provide for them, or love them. You plied them with false affections and gifts, gaining their trust and loyalty. Then you abused them. Mental, physical, and sexual abuse. What kind of monster does that? Modern media calls it grooming. I do not care for the term. The word does not describe the seriousness of your crime. You rape children. You are a truly despicable man!"

Farid stared at me, his expression blank. The man held no shame, no remorse for his cruel behaviour. I leapt to my feet, my anger causing me to shake as I stepped towards him and raised my fist.

"Boss!" Franco yelled as he grabbed my arm before I could strike Farid. "Not until we get what we need."

I shook away Franco's firm grip and took a step back from Farid.

Franco was right. There would be time to make him suffer after we got the information we needed.

Turning towards the curtained window, I tried to regain my composure. I needed a drink—something to calm the storm raging through my mind.

I picked up my phone from the lamp table and called who I hoped would be our ace in the uncooperative hand we'd been dealt.

"Can you come in here and bring me a scotch on the rocks? Make it a double. Thanks, Rashid." After placing my phone back on the lamp table, I sat across from my prisoner and waited.

After two silent minutes, there was a knock on the door. Franco opened it and let Rashid inside.

"Mr Ali, let me introduce you to my London-based technical security advisor, Rashid Khan."

Rashid handed me my drink and stood beside my chair, his arms folded, almost mirroring Franco's stance.

"Do you recognise anything familiar about Rashid's clothing, Mr Ali?" I asked, watching with ill-concealed satisfaction as Farid took in Rashid's appearance. Farid's coat fit Rashid like it was made for him, and he wore boot-cut jeans that were the same shade and brand as those Farid had arrived in.

"As you can see, your likeness to my employee is uncanny, even down to the way you groom your facial hair. I must admit, Rashid received some teasing when he first grew his beard. What was it Jonesy said to you, Rashid?"

"He told me his old aunt Ruth had more beard than me."

"To which you replied?"

"That's why she was the main attraction in the travelling circus."

"Ahh, yes, I remember that now. You and Jonesy have a very odd sense of humour. I don't know how your commanding officer put up with both of you being in the same unit."

"Neither does he, boss. He said so the last time our old unit got together."

"I know that Jonesy and Franco filled you in yesterday regarding the nature of Mr Ali and his friends' interest in young girls."

"They did, boss. Made me sick to my stomach."

"As it would any decent human being," I conceded, agreeing with Rashid. "But earlier, Mr Ali tried to tell Franco and me that these young girls deserved what they did to them because they were not of his culture and weren't Muslim. Being a Muslim man yourself, Rashid, tell me what you think about the claims he made?"

"He disgusts me. How dare he use my religion to try and justify such heinous acts? My culture and religion would never condone manipulating children like that. It amazes me why so many Muslims choose to live in a free Western society when they supposedly despise the way Westerners choose to live. I have daughters and—"

"How can you call yourself a Muslim? From what this man said, you fought in the British Army, likely in Iraq or Afghanistan—fighting fellow Muslims. It's you who committed the heinous acts, but they were against Allah, not just stupid white bitches," Farid yelled.

I placed a hand on Rashid's arm to steady him. I could almost feel the anger building within him, yet outwardly he looked calm. He and Jonesy were similar in that way, as was Franco. True soldiers. You would only ever see what they allowed, no matter how they felt on the inside.

I wish I could keep up the detached appearance I'd started with, but I had already shown how easily I'd become affected by the evil before me. It was time to up my game and fight fire with fire.

"Mr Ali, earlier you said the police would come looking for you when your friends raised the alarm. You mentioned GPS and CCTV. Rashid, why don't you tell Mr Ali what you did this afternoon?"

"Franco and Don apprehended Mr Ali when he

approached the lifts about ten minutes after he'd entered the hotel. They brought him to this room and stripped him before cable-tying him to the chair. Then Don brought me his coat and phone, and we discussed the best way to make it look like Mr Ali had left the building. I spoke to Kevin about monitoring CCTV and told him the route I'd be taking. After putting on Mr Ali's coat, I made my way over to Starbucks on Oxford Street, where I purchased a latte. Before leaving Starbucks, I called Kevin to let him know it was time. He hacked into, then disabled, CCTV on Oxford Street, allowing me to remove Mr Ali's coat without it being on camera. Then I turned off GPS tracking on his phone and removed the SIM before stashing it in a carrier bag, along with the coat. Kevin let me know when he'd disabled each CCTV on my planned route back to Mayfair, allowing me to return to the hotel without a trace."

"So let me see if I've got this right. According to CCTV and GPS tracking on Mr Ali's phone, his last known location was Starbucks on Oxford Street?" I asked, although I already knew the answer.

"Yes, boss, that's correct."

"So, Mr Ali, it appears your earlier assumption that your friends and the police would be able to find you was incorrect. Now tell me, how does it feel to know you have no control over this situation? That you have no choice but to give us the information we require to gain your freedom?"

"I'm not a fucking idiot. You've got me tied to a chair on plastic sheets, so my blood doesn't stain the carpet. You've no intention of letting me go, whether I give you information or not. You wouldn't have gone to all those lengths to make it look like I'd left the hotel if you were going to let me live. Well, I've got news for you. I'm saying nothing about that ginger-haired bitch we were looking for, or her slutty friend. So fuck you, whoever you are."

Both Rashid and Franco glanced my way, silently asking if they should step in and beat the man for his disrespect. I shook my head.

"Rashid, you can go now. I appreciate your help today."

Rashid nodded, then turned to leave. When he reached the door, he turned back around and said, "Boss, make him suffer."

15

KOLYA

When the door closed behind Rashid, I drank the rest of my scotch and placed the empty glass on the table. I made a show of looking at my watch—as if what would happen in this room meant nothing at all to me.

"Let me introduce myself to you, Mr Ali. I realise now it was remiss of me not to do so earlier. My name is Kolya Barinov. I do not expect you to recognise my name; it is my business that people are more familiar with. I am the owner of KOLCAT Engineering: a company that designs, manufactures, and trades in weapons and defence aids. We have been in the news recently due to the expansion of one of our manufacturing plants in the UK. The headlines were extremely favourable, saying we were responsible for the biggest boost in employment and the economy that this country has seen in over forty years. Of course, there were those who mentioned us selling to the Saudis and various other countries people weren't happy with, but one cannot take the good without the bad—wouldn't you agree?"

I observed him carefully, watching for any sign that he recalled what I'd been talking about. A sliver of satisfaction flowed through me when recognition appeared on his face. The manufacturing plant in question was only around thirty miles from where Farid lived, so he could not have failed to hear about it.

"I also own this hotel—in case you were wondering. And this setup"—I gestured towards him and at the plastic sheeting—"is nothing new to me. My father has been a pakhan in the Russian mob since before I was born. His methods of extracting information are brutal, yet effective. Though today I would prefer not to bloody my hotel more than I need to. So, Mr Ali, I ask you again. Why were you and your friends searching for Tess Robertson, and where is Sarah Crowther?"

Farid licked his dry lips and stared at me through his one good eye. He took a deep breath in and, for a moment, I thought he would answer my questions. Instead of doing that—which would have given him a relatively quick death—he laughed, then yelled, "*FUCK. YOU.*"

In less than two seconds, I stood before him, my fists raining down on his face and body. The cacophony of sounds that came from fists hitting flesh, the breaking of bones, and blood splattering against plastic built to a sickening crescendo, along with the ever-increasing cries of Farid Ali's pain.

I beat him until he was barely conscious, then I stepped back to allow Franco to rouse him by throwing cold water in his swollen face and down the back of his neck.

I walked back to my chair, adrenaline making my heart beat faster. My hands felt odd, like they were too heavy for my arms, and I'd split the skin over two of my knuckles. I knew I should get some ice to counteract the swelling that would soon appear, but there wasn't time for it. My patience with this man, and with this whole situation, was non-existent. If he still did not answer my questions, then I would resort to my backup plan—to threats that I, both as a father, *and* as a man who puts great value into the innocence of childhood, did not care to use.

"So, Mr Ali, do you feel like answering my questions now?" I asked, silently praying that he would, for all our sakes.

"Fuck. You," he wheezed before spitting out blood and saliva, along with a tooth.

Damn! I did not want to do this, but I had no choice. *He* had given me no choice.

I picked up my phone and read the message that brought me up to speed with what I needed to know from my team. They'd been watching over Tess's foster mother up in Doncaster until earlier today. I looked towards Franco, who nodded his head before opening the door. My iPad and other items I knew we would need if it got this far were outside where I'd left them.

As soon as I had the iPad in my hands, I played the video I received earlier, resting the device on the side table in plain view of my prisoner.

"Do you recognise anyone in this video, Mr Ali?" I asked, knowing full well what his answer would be.

"What the...? That's my wife, my son and my daughter. Where are they? What have you done with them? If you've hurt them, I'll—"

"You'll what, Mr Ali? Escape your bindings to save them —bloody and broken as you are? Come now, would you have me believe that you have superpowers, like the character in the Xbox game your son is currently playing?"

I quickly changed the video from the one filmed earlier, when Farid's wife picked up his son from school to the live feed from outside his house. As the curtains were open, my men had a clear view inside the property. Currently, his son was concentrating on the video game he was playing as his mother watched over him, her daughter asleep in her arms.

"As you can guess, Mr Ali, my business takes me all over the world. I have extremely wealthy, if not always *honourable,* clients. Child trafficking has always been a profitable business, and one I think you've enjoyed the spoils of for some time."

"I haven't, I swear. I've never been into trafficking children," he wailed.

"No?" I questioned, leaning forward in my chair to bring us closer. "From what I've heard, you and your friends thought nothing of taking vulnerable young girls from a place of safety into a den of sick and twisted men. To my understanding, Sarah told you how upset she was at your request that she kiss and pleasure these men, yet you used your influence *and* her desperation to be loved to get her to comply. You trafficked without fully exchanging the girl until you feared she was going to trap you with a child."

"No! She wasn't trafficked. I wouldn't do that."

"So you think you are a better person because you didn't add the trafficking label to what you did? Sarah is still missing! If you haven't passed her on to someone else, then you are keeping her hidden. To what end, I can only guess. Tell me where she is. NOW. Or I will give the order to have my men enter your house and take your children."

"No. No, please, not my children," he cried, sobbing in between ongoing pleas to save his family.

I asked again, in a calm voice this time, "Where is Sarah Crowther, and why were you searching for Tess Robertson?"

"Sarah's dead. Hassan killed her," he sobbed, shaking his head as if trying to deny the truth behind his words.

"It wasn't meant to go that far. We were only going to threaten her—maybe slap her around a bit. But Hassan lost his temper when she said she was pregnant. He told her she was a whore, not fit to raise a child, then he started punching her in her belly. She fell to her knees, and Hassan dove on her. He grabbed her hair and used it to keep slamming her head onto the concrete floor. Me and Tariq tried to stop him, but he fought us off. Then he went for her throat. I don't know whether she was already dead before he attempted to strangle her, but by the time we got him to let go, she was gone."

In my mind, I already feared she was dead, but to hear the circumstances of how it happened, of how a fifteen-year-old girl had her life cut short in such a horrific way… I had no words for how sickened and devastated I was feeling. I looked to Franco, not knowing what else to do in those gut-wrenching moments as my mind played out the terrible scene Farid had just described.

Franco looked back at me and shook his head. He let out a sigh, then cleared his throat before saying to Farid, “You were two grown men. You could have stopped this Hassan guy from hurting her, but you didn’t. You wanted her dead as much as he did.”

“No, I swear, we were only supposed to scare her. But Hassan…we can’t always stop him. He’s a loose cannon, he—”

“Are you saying this has happened before?” Franco yelled. “Has he killed another young girl?”

Farid became silent again. He stared at the floor, avoiding both my and Franco’s angry glare.

I picked up my phone and dialled through to my team outside Farid’s home, putting it on speakerphone so Farid could hear.

“Sean, be ready to go in and take the children. We don’t need the wife. Dispose of her as you see fit.”

“No, don’t, please…I swear I’ll tell you everything; just leave my family alone. I was going to answer. I mean it. Please.”

“Sean, stand down for now. Our captive has decided to cooperate.”

“Boss,” Sean replied in confirmation.

I should be happy that Farid had taken the bait—believing I was ruthless enough to take children from the arms of their mother. The thought was abhorrent to me. I would never follow through with such an act. But after discussing the situation with my team, we decided we could use this form of deception as a backup plan. For it to work, Farid Ali had to love his children and want them safe and happy, even though he wouldn't be around to see them grow. It was a shame he didn't feel that other children deserved the same happiness and safety.

"I am willing to spare your wife and leave your children alone *if* you reveal the details of all members of your grooming ring, the adults and children involved—including any who are deceased—and the properties you took them to. I want to know the whereabouts of Sarah Crowther's body, plus any others you know of, and lastly, I want to know why you were searching for Tess Robertson. I want all this recorded in both voice and written form. To film you so beaten and bloody would invite too many questions. If you comply with my request, your family will have nothing to fear from me."

Both Franco and I breathed a sigh of relief when Farid nodded and said, "I'll do it."

16

KOLYA

I ran the completed recording through a speech-to-text device before sending the text to a printer—being careful that the paper was handled by gloved hands only.

After Farid had signed and dated the papers, I gave Franco a nod and watched as he swiftly broke the man's neck. For his crimes, he deserved a long, drawn-out, torturous death, but I wanted his body gone so I could get back to the hospital to stay with Tess. Only, once it was over and done with, it didn't feel right to be in her presence.

Although the man deserved it, it was I who had ordered his death, and I would carry that with me for the rest of my days. I felt unclean, as if tainted by my actions, or by knowing the full extent of the crimes those despicable men had committed. Crimes I decided to keep from Tess until it was safe to reveal them.

Another reason I could not face her tonight.

Tess was desperate for information about her friend, but the trauma of finding out they'd murdered Sarah might set back her recovery—something I could not allow to happen. The sooner Tess healed, the restricting metaphysical band around my chest might loosen, allowing me to breathe easier. I needed that to happen. Knowing she'd been so hurt while saving my life left me with the strangest feelings. At least that's what I think had caused them.

The need to protect her and keep her safe was a given. I could understand that. And to make sure she was financially secure—a just reward, I would say. It was the need to keep her close, to touch her, possess her even. *That* was something I had a hard time understanding. Not to mention when I'd done nothing more than kiss her cheek while she slept, I felt more at peace than I have for many years.

She wasn't yet eighteen—nearly two years younger than my son, who was currently studying in America. Tess needed to finish her education, see the world, and fall in love.

Why did thinking about Tess falling in love with someone make me feel so empty inside?

I placed the recording and letter Farid Ali had composed into a sealed Jiffy envelope and clear plastic bag, then allowed myself to take off the surgical gloves. There would be no fingerprints to trace this information back to me or my men.

My phone alerted me to an incoming message. Ivan had the helicopter ready, and his flight back to Oxford had been cleared for take-off.

Jonesy and Franco placed Farid Ali's body in a large, rolling laundry hamper and were making their way to the helipad.

Lucas took a call, and then came to stand by my side.

"Boss, Jack says he's got everything ready. He'll start the fire when they call to let him know they're ten minutes from landing, so it will be burning well by the time they arrive. Franco and Jack will stay and make sure there's nothing left of the body but ash."

"Thank you, Lucas. Tell Franco and Ivan to stay in Oxford; there's no need for them to fly back tonight. They may as well sleep in their own beds. Just have them here in the morning to bring Tess home from the hospital. Today has been stressful for all of us, and I appreciate how hard it was to coordinate everything at such short notice. Rest assured, I will reward you for your efforts."

Lucas nodded; his brow furrowed as if deep in thought when he turned to walk away. When he got to the door, he turned back around to face me.

"We all appreciate how generous you are, boss, but I don't just speak for myself when I say consider today a freebie. The only reward I'd like is to see those other sick bastards burning with him."

After Lucas left, I placed the bag containing the information Farid Ali supplied in my safe. Even though my suite at the hotel differed completely from the room where we'd held, then killed him, I could almost see the image of Farid tied to the chair, his head lolling over at a strange angle.

I'd witnessed death many times in Russia. My father's business saw to that. I first killed a man when I was just eleven years old. Gunmen had opened fire on the car in which my mother and I travelled home from church. One of our guards took a bullet to the temple; his dead body slumping over my mother most likely saved her life.

There were automatic rifles underneath the seats, so I'd joined the other guard who'd rode with us, firing back at the men who attacked us. My father had taught us, when using automatic rifles, one should always revert to the *"spray and pray"* approach if there was limited opportunity to take aim. With that first round, I'd put a bullet in a man's forehead and hit the arm of another. My mother was screaming for me to get down, but I wouldn't do so until I eradicated the threat. That kill was different. It was self-defence.

The memory of that day caused adrenaline to rush through me. My head started pounding—the scotch I was drinking not helping matters. I brought myself back to the here and now by recalling the reason Farid said they'd been searching for Tess. She'd had Sarah's iPhone, which contained photos of all three of the men, plus others. And they weren't sure how much incriminating information Sarah had told her.

They planned to take Tess to a house in Nottingham, drug her, and have men use her for sex for a month or two before killing her. They were going to make it look like an overdose, then dump her body in a river.

Suddenly, the image of the sick bastard's dead body didn't

seem so disturbing. If anything, I found it almost pleasing. Only now, I regretted not making him suffer more than he had, and wished it was I, not Franco, who'd taken his life with my bare hands.

17

TESS

I should have been happy to be deemed well enough to leave the hospital, but as the car I was travelling in pulled up outside the hotel Kolya owned, I couldn't help the anxiety and fear taking over my whole being.

Nate and Kolya sat in the back of the vehicle with me, and Franco and Lucas travelled in the front. Because of the privacy screen, I wasn't sure which of them was driving.

Kolya appeared calm as he tried to make conversation, pointing out a few billboards advertising West End shows I might enjoy. Nate, on the other hand, had been busy studying people outside our vehicle every time we stopped in traffic. His large, muscular frame appeared tense—as if he expected to spring into action at any moment. Neither Kolya nor Nate had commented on my apparent nervousness.

There was also a security team in the car following us, but

none of my worries were about the reasons they were required. The actual reason for my crippling anxiety was waiting for me on the hotel's roof.

A guard I recognised as Jonesy came towards the car as Nate opened the door. Out of nowhere, a line of men made a kind of man alleyway while Nate and Franco hustled us through the hotel foyer and into a lift.

Kolya had his left hand pressed firmly against my lower back from leaving the car until we were inside the lift, as if he was expecting me to fall back at any moment. His right hand was bandaged due to an accident he'd had the night before. When I'd asked what he'd done, he told me it was nothing. He'd been more concerned about getting me home.

My shoulder ached from getting in and out of the car, although Kolya and Nate ensured I had all the help I needed. I focused on the pain to avoid thinking about the helicopter ride, but Kolya told me he had a surprise for me in his suite.

We stepped out of the elevator into a minimally-furnished room with only two black leather club chairs and a few gilt-framed paintings on its burgundy walls.

Kolya took my hand and led me through a double doorway into another room. And there, on a sofa opposite a large fire-place, sat Danny, with Bess wagging her tail exuberantly at his feet.

I dashed over to them, intending to hug Danny as he stood up to greet me. With only one good arm and the other being supported in a sling, the hug was awkward, although no less heartfelt.

"Steady, Tess," Danny said as he put his hand on my good arm to support me.

"What are you doing here?" I asked, lowering myself into a squatting position so I could fuss Bess.

"Careful," Kolya cautioned as he came towards us and bent to help me up.

"Someone called Franco came to find me, to let me know what had happened to you. I was really worried, Tess, and I couldn't believe you'd been shot. I asked him if he'd let me know how you were doing because I knew they wouldn't let me in the hospital with Bess. Then about an hour later, Franco came back and said someone called Mr Barinov—who was taking care of you—said I could spend a few nights at his hotel so I could get cleaned up properly and come and see you, while someone there looked after Bess. I was dubious at first, but I wanted to see for myself that you were going to be okay, so I went with him and ended up here."

It was then that I let myself really look at him. He looked cleaner and had shaved; his wavy blond hair was much shorter. He wore smart grey trousers and a blue V-neck sweater over a white shirt. Even Bess, the black wire-haired terrier, looked like she'd been bathed and groomed.

I'd had tears in my eyes since I'd first spotted them, as had Danny, but it wasn't until I turned to thank Kolya for finding and helping him that the tears fell.

Kolya pulled me close and gave me a kiss on top of my head while I cried and said, "Thank you."

"Don't cry, *malyutka*; it is all good news. Danny has agreed to join my security. He'll be travelling by car with the rest of my team after we leave. He's moving into the staff quarters with little Bess, so you will get to see him often."

I looked at Danny, who was smiling at Kolya as he finished speaking. Taking his PTSD into account, I wondered how that would work, but I said nothing. I was just so glad to be seeing my friend again, and there was no way I was going to spoil this opportunity for him.

I turned when I heard someone clear their throat behind us and saw Nate putting his phone in the inside pocket of his tailored black suit jacket.

"Boss, they've given us clearance to leave twenty minutes earlier than planned if you'd like to take advantage of it."

"Good," replied Kolya. "Come, Tess, let's make our way to the helipad. The sooner we are home, the sooner you can rest."

I nodded and tried to smile as the fear I'd forgotten when I'd spotted Danny and Bess reared its ugly head once again.

We ascended to the rooftop. The rotor blades of the helicopter were already spinning when the doors of the lift opened and... I froze. Kolya's hand was on my back, urging me forward, but I couldn't move or even breathe. The sounds, the force of the draft, and even the sight of the huge helicopter kept me immobile.

Kolya, Nate, and Jonesy all stopped and turned to look at me in surprise.

"What's wrong, *malyutka*?" asked Kolya, leaning down to get his mouth level with my ear so I could hear him above the deafening noise.

"I can't do it," I shouted, stepping further back inside the lift.

"What do you mean? What's wrong, Tess?" Kolya asked again, concern and worry wrinkling his brow.

"I just can't get in it. I've never flown before. What if I'm sick, or we crash or, or…"

"Shh," whispered Kolya in my ear. "Don't panic, *malyutka*. We will take a moment. Don't worry yourself." He moved away from me slightly and shouted something to Nate and Jonesy. Then he stepped back into the lift and closed the doors.

"Tess, I'm sorry. I didn't know you were feeling so nervous about flying. I should have talked to you about all this before."

"No, I'm sorry," I replied, sniffling.

God, when did I become such a crier? I could count on one hand how many times I'd cried in the last ten years before all this happened. And three of those were when I'd seen animals die in films, like *Old Yeller* and *Marley & Me*. *E.T.* did it for me every time, too. The only humans I'd ever cried about were Jean—when she'd had her heart attack—and the old lady from next door to her when she'd died. Never for myself, or any situation I found myself in.

"Tess, you can do this. You are a brave and strong young woman. You have survived some terrible things in the past and lived to tell the tale, so you will easily get through the short flight to my home. Do you really believe I would allow you or my staff to fly if it wasn't safe to do so? And do you think I would willingly put you in danger when you saved my life and nearly lost your own in the process?"

I shook my head and met his ice-blue eyes, momentarily mesmerised by the emotion in them. Kolya kept his eyes locked with mine as he pulled my body gently into his and held me against him, putting his arms around me carefully so as not to hurt my wound.

"Tess, you are shaking," he stated, his voice full of concern. "Please don't be afraid. I will keep you safe. I will *always* keep you safe, *malyutka*. Never doubt that."

My knees went weak, my heartbeat raced through my chest, and when I tried to swallow, it felt like I had something in my throat. But it wasn't through fear this time. No, not fear at all. It was the feeling of being held so close by this handsome, strong, caring man that made my heart flutter and my head spin.

I closed my eyes, took a slow, steadying breath, and then looked up to meet his concerned gaze.

"Okay," I almost whispered. "I'll do it. Go in the helicopter, I mean."

He grinned in that slow, sexy way I'd seen him do over the last few days, then kissed me on the tip of my nose, and I swear I almost swooned. I would have been happy to stay that way forever, but Kolya turned and pressed the button to open the doors.

The noise and draft from the helicopter filled my ears again, but I didn't have time to think about it as he ushered me towards the open door of the flying blue beast.

Nate got inside first and reached down to place his hand

under my good arm, while Kolya placed a hand over my ribs on my left-hand side, helping me step inside the surprisingly spacious aircraft.

I'd been expecting something like I'd seen on TV—in the helicopter rescue series with the air ambulance—but it wasn't anything like that.

This was pure luxury.

Two rows of three comfortable tan leather seats faced each other. The seat opened up mechanically in the middle of one row, revealing a small bar with water bottles and various wines and spirits. The walls were a rich cream, and a matching carpet that my feet sank into covered the floor.

Kolya, Nate, Jonesy, and Franco joined me in the helicopter, and I wondered whether Ivan was flying. The seating area was closed off from where the pilots were, so I couldn't tell.

Kolya held my hand as the helicopter lifted away, and it surprised me how smoothly it rose into the air. I'd been expecting a jolt or some pulling feeling, but other than the small vibrations as we left the helipad, there wasn't anything notable. It wasn't until the helicopter veered slightly to the left that I experienced a swooping feeling, similar to being on a fairground ride like the Waltzer, but with much less force.

I gripped Kolya's hand even tighter and took a deep breath. He made sure the seat belt I wore wasn't too constrictive when I leaned forward a little so I could see all the capital's landmarks he was pointing out.

Gradually, the landmarks got smaller, and soon we were flying over seemingly endless stretches of motorway. The view turned more pleasant when we flew over green fields and woodland.

Nate winked and told me it wouldn’t be long until we arrived, and I was genuinely surprised by how quick and pleasant our journey had been, and how much I'd enjoyed it.

18

TESS

Coming in to land wasn't as bad as I imagined it would be. Maybe it was because Kolya held my hand tight in his, or it could have been because I was taking in the sight of his home for the first time.

Kolya's house appeared to be built in the middle of nowhere and was surrounded by fields and woodland. The façade of his home was an old stone-built manor house, but as we neared the helipad, I could see that the old house had a U-shaped extension around the back. In the middle of the U was a swimming pool, and what looked like a basketball court.

"Welcome home," Kolya said while carefully unfastening the safety belt. I must have looked a little worried by his words because he quickly added, "This will be your home for as long as you want or need it, *malyutka*, and everyone here will make sure you are safe and well cared for."

Nate helped me out of the helicopter, leading me quickly into the back of the house. We walked through a small, sparsely furnished porch into a large, modern kitchen with a huge dining table set with plates of buffet-style food. A pretty woman with short grey hair stepped away from the table and approached me.

"Hello, you must be Tess. I would hug you or shake your hand, but I don't want to hurt you, and I bet your injury is aching after your journey. My name is Nancy, but you can call me Nan. All this lot do."

Nate bent forward and kissed her on the side of her cheek.

"I'm Kolya's housekeeper, and my husband, Jack, is the gardener," Nan informed me, pointing to a man who was approaching us. Jack had no qualms about taking my hand and shaking it.

"Pleased to meet you, Tess," he said with a beaming smile. Nan and Jack appeared to be in their early sixties, and I immediately felt at ease with both of them.

"I'll show you to your room, and when you're ready, you can come and get something to eat. I wouldn't leave it too long, though. These men are always hungry, and Ivan seems to eat for three," Nan told me with a chuckle.

"How long have you worked for Kolya?" I asked as she led me down a hallway.

"They brought me in when James was born, though not as a nanny. His mother was very hands-on and wanted to be a full-time mum. They had staff already, so I was just someone extra to help when needed. Jack came to work for Kolya when he left the army, so I knew the family anyway. My son had cystic fibrosis and passed away after a severe bout of pneumonia when he was twelve, so being around James was a balm for my heart and soul. I like to think I was the same for him when his mother died. I've missed him so much since he's been in the States, and I'm counting down the days until he's home for his birthday."

"I'm sorry to hear about your son, Nan," I said when we stopped outside a door.

"Thank you, Tess. He's in a better place now, without all the pain and suffering, and I know we'll meet again in heaven. In the meantime, I have all these boys to look after, no matter how grown up they are." She opened the door and gestured for me to enter.

The room was painted in a pale cream shade and was furnished with a double bed, a tall chest of drawers, a four-door wardrobe and two bedside cabinets.

Even with all the light oak furniture, it was spacious. The bed, in particular, was something that drew the eye. At the head of the bed, from what I could see over the pillows, were exquisitely detailed wooden leaves climbing up the central five spindles, and the posts at each corner were shaped like acorns. The same leaf and acorn design echoed throughout the rest of the furniture, and the overall effect gave the room a cosy cottage feel. Both the bed linen and curtains were a slightly darker cream than the walls. A patchwork comforter in various shades of cream, sage green, and taupe—along with two matching throw cushions—broke up the plain colours perfectly.

"If you don't like anything in here, *malyutka*, we can

always change it. It's only ever been a guest room, so if it's not to your taste, you can change anything you wish."

I turned to find Kolya in the doorway. He was looking at me expectantly. As if I would tell him I wanted new curtains or a new bed. I wouldn't dream of saying anything like that, even if I didn't think it was so beautiful and homely that I wanted to lie on the bed and marvel at everything in here. Kolya paid for me to have private healthcare, brought me to his home to recover, and vowed to keep me safe from the men who were pursuing me—as well as offering my friend a job. I wasn't an ungrateful bitch, and I'm not an idiot, either. You don't *"bite the hand that feeds,"* as the saying goes.

"It's beautiful," I answered truthfully. Kolya nodded and watched while Nan led me through a doorway on the left side of the room, which turned out to be an en-suite bathroom. Inside there was a separate bath and shower that seemed quite modern in design, as opposed to the bedroom furniture—although the beige marbled tiles had a similar leaf design bordering them. The sink and toilet spanned one wall and had integrated cupboards surrounding them in a glossy cream finish. There were two towels hung over a heated towel rail, and Nan showed me which cupboards held more.

"I'll unpack your things if you want to go and get something to eat, Tess," Nan announced. She walked over to where Kolya had placed my bags from the hospital.

"No, that's okay," I answered quickly. I wanted to show these people I was no slacker and could earn my keep.

"If I have an early night, I'm sure I'll be able to help you with the housework. Maybe some dusting and wiping around the kitchen? Then, when my wound is better, I can have some proper duties."

I heard Nan gasp, and Kolya looked so angry that I stepped back until my legs hit the bed. He stalked towards me, glaring, but closed his eyes when he came to a stop in front of me. He took a deep, calming breath before opening his eyes again.

"Do you think I brought you here to work for me?"

I shook my head, gesturing around the room and to the clothes I wore. "But you've been so generous, Kolya, and I have nothing to give you in return."

"Did I do or say anything that led you to believe you needed to pay me, Tess? Do you think I only brought you here because I needed a cleaner?"

"No. Not really, I… Kolya, I don't know what to make of all this. And I don't know how to deal with it. With all your kindness and generosity, I mean."

It was the truth. Jean had been kind and generous with her time, but that had been taken away from me. There was a little voice at the back of my head saying, "*Any minute now, it will all be taken away again.*" I suppose I thought if I was useful and worked for my keep, I had more of a chance of staying around.

Kolya placed his forehead against mine and sighed. "Tess, I've not brought you here to work. But I don't want you to feel uncomfortable with the situation, either. Will you promise me that for the next eight weeks, you will just relax and recuperate? Then we can discuss further what will make you more agreeable to accepting my help."

"Okay," I answered, although, with his forehead against mine and our bodies in such close proximity, I would have agreed to anything he asked.

Never before had I been affected by a male in this way—be it man or boy. The opposite sex used to make me feel nervous, and hearing the noises they made when my mother took them to her room made me feel physically ill. So what had suddenly changed?

Kolya was an extremely good-looking man. He had a face and body a film star would be proud of, but he was way too old for me.

He could probably have his pick of sexy, sophisticated women too, so it was silly of me to develop feelings for him. I was a nobody in the grand scheme of things. Just a random teenage runaway he felt indebted to. My frizzy coppery hair and too many freckles meant I couldn't pull off a sophisticated look, and my past gave me way too much baggage for even the strongest man to carry. So I would have to be content to stay in his shadow and accept whatever scraps he offered until I could branch out on my own.

Kolya said he'd give me a good life in return for saving his, and I believed him. But giving Danny a job and providing free room and board for me was payment enough.

Kolya took my hand and led me back to the kitchen. It turned out that Nan was a skilled cook, and most of the buffet was home-made. I chose pasta with tuna, mayo, sweetcorn, and salad. I'd barely begun to eat when Ivan handed over a plate of vegetable samosas and mushroom pakoras before sitting opposite me. He said nothing, just nodded his head in approval when I placed one of each on my plate.

Kolya sat beside me, and Nate and another guy named Kevin sat beside him. Then Lucas came to the table with Nan's husband. They each grabbed a plate and selected a few things from the many on offer.

I don't know what I'd expected, but everyone sitting around the table together and chatting like good friends wasn't it. It was almost as if Kolya wasn't their employer, and the informal setting and friendly atmosphere made me feel more at ease.

I asked if any of them lived on the estate and was surprised to find they all did. Other than Nate, Kevin, Nan and Jack, all the staff lived in the old manor. Kolya lived in the new extension, and his bedroom was next to mine.

Nate and Kevin lived in the opposite part of the extension to Kolya. Kevin operated the computer systems that ran the cameras and kept the estate secure. By his own admission, he said he was a geek, but looking at him from where I sat, he didn't quite fit the stereotype. He was tall with an athletic build, shoulder-length shaggy blond hair and deep-blue eyes. I imagined he had girls throwing themselves at him. But then I looked over at Lucas, Nate and Ivan and realised I was sitting with some of the most handsome men I'd ever seen. Yet none of them made my knees weak like Kolya. He just had that certain something extra. Something I couldn't quite identify, but was there all the same.

Nan was fussing around everyone, making sure they had

enough to eat and asking what they wanted to drink. She seemed like such a warm-hearted woman and obviously adored these guys. They all enjoyed her motherly nature, too, by the look of it.

19

TESS

My first night in Kolya's home was so different from what I'd expected. Although my surroundings were new to me, I felt at ease with everyone, and my bed was the comfiest I'd ever slept in.

Whether it was exhaustion from travelling after just being discharged from the hospital, or the pain medication they sent me home with, I slept like the dead—only waking when Kolya came to check on me with a cup of tea. I'd slept for ten hours, and my upper body felt still and awkward when I sat up in bed.

Kolya helped me get comfortable before bringing me breakfast in bed. I loved being pampered by him, but I still felt like a bit of a spare part when neither he nor Nan let me wash my breakfast plates.

While getting dressed, I found myself with a bit of a dilemma. A nurse helped me put on my clothes before I left the hospital, and as I'd worn a button-up blouse and cardigan, they'd been easy to take off. I hadn't needed the help Nan offered at all.

She'd hung up all the new clothes Kolya bought me after I arrived, and from them, I'd selected an oyster-pink long-sleeved Henley top. Wearing a bra was out of the question until my wound healed.

Kolya had taken the sizes of the clothes they'd cut from me before they operated and sent them to his assistant. Due to hardly eating while living on the streets of London, most of the clothing his assistant had chosen was quite loose, which I'd appreciated when I struggled to put the top on. I selected a pair of pink lace knickers and added navy-blue yoga pants to complete my outfit.

Kolya bought me a pair of suede ankle boots to travel home in yesterday and a pair of slip-on trainers, which I knew I would live in, as they were the most comfortable footwear I had ever owned.

After putting on the trainers, I thought about heading to the kitchen to see Kolya again, but a sudden bout of dizziness and fatigue almost knocked me off my feet. All the effort of getting dressed as carefully as possible while still feeling pain had taken its toll on me, so I lay down on the bed to rest for a few minutes.

There was a knock at the door, so I shouted for whoever it was to come in. Kolya opened the door, smiling broadly, but immediately became concerned.

"Tess, are you all right? You look so pale again."

"I think getting dressed has taken it out of me. Give me a few minutes, and I'll be okay."

"Nonsense, *malyutka*. You will rest for an hour or two, at least. Are you in any pain?"

"A little. It was more awkward putting my clothes on than taking them off."

"Then you should have accepted my or Nan's help. Promise me, Tess, that when getting dressed or undressed, you will let us be around to help in case you have difficulties. The same goes for bathing. I know you said you would have a bath tonight, so when you do, let one of us be around in case you need help getting in or out."

"I've told Nan she can wait in here while I get out in case I find it too difficult. She said she'd help me re-apply the dressing, so I don't have to worry about keeping it dry. That means I could have a shower instead."

"How about washing your hair? Do you think you can lift your arm enough?"

"The nurse washed my hair again at the hospital yesterday morning. I don't normally wash it more than three times a week due to how long it takes to keep my curls under control afterwards."

"Okay, well, when it's time to wash it again, you can let Nan help you. I would hate for you to fall because you made yourself dizzy by doing things your body is not ready to do without help. How about I bring in my laptop so you can choose clothes that are easier to put on while your movement is restricted?"

"I'll manage with the clothes I have, Kolya. You've spent too much on me already."

"Tess, you cannot just have the handful of items my assistant brought you. And you must not worry about me spending money on you. I will do it often, so you need to get used to it. Now, shall I leave you to sleep for a while, or are you ready to do some shopping online?"

"I'm not sleepy, Kolya, but I'm not sure about shopping online. It's not something I've ever done. I don't even have a proper bank account, never mind a bank card. I know Jean used to do her supermarket shopping online sometimes, and she used her card to pay. But I just…."

I sighed heavily, feeling so out of my depth in the life I now found myself living.

"Tess, we will take our time, and I will show you everything you need to know about online shopping. I'm sure it will be something you enjoy once you get used to it. How about I bring us a hot drink before we attempt to fill your wardrobe?"

Kolya laughed at the horrified look on my face.

"Oh, Tess, you may be the only woman I have ever known who doesn't want to buy new clothes. I promise it will not be so bad."

He took my hand and kissed it before frowning.

"You are not wearing your sling, *malyutka*. You must wear it at all times during the day. Let me help you put it on."

I told him I hadn't put it on yet because I'd just got dressed, but I'd actually forgotten about it. He was careful when he helped me sit up so I could slip it on, and I found myself enjoying his touch as he adjusted it for me. When he left the room to get his laptop and our drinks, I couldn't wait for him to return. Not for the shopping, but because I enjoyed being in his company.

I wasn't sure how long he'd want me to stay here with him, but I hoped it'd be far longer than my recovery would take. I felt at home here, but it had nothing to do with the building. It was Kolya himself who made me feel safe and secure enough to relax in my new surroundings.

Kolya asked me to choose which stores I wanted to shop from, and I hesitated with my reply. So he picked up his mobile phone and asked whomever he spoke to what were the most popular stores that young women preferred. It turned out that Greta—his assistant—recommended Top Shop, River Island, and Vivian Westwood.

Now, I know I'm not the best person to ask about fashion, but I'm pretty sure that Vivian Westwood is way out of most girls' budgets—especially where I come from. However, Kolya wouldn't be deterred, and pretty soon, he was buying everything I expressed interest in. So I stopped telling him I liked something, hoping he'd slow down. He didn't.

Regarding jeans, I've never been sure what leg length I need, so Kolya brought Nan in with a tape measure. At five foot four, most things—including the yoga pants I was wearing—were always slightly too long for me. Nan measured my inside leg at twenty-nine inches, then proceeded to measure the rest of me, including my bust. I blushed when she remarked that I wasn't wearing a bra and was glad that Kolya had the decency to look away. He seemed uncomfortable, and I didn't know how to take that. It should have made me happy that a man wasn't interested in my boobs, but truthfully, I felt a little disappointed.

Kolya wrote down all my measurements, leaving Nan and me to choose new underwear and nightwear, which she insisted were from Marks and Spencer. "You can never go wrong with M&S knickers," she stated.

Kolya returned ten minutes later with a glass of water and one of the antibiotics the hospital sent me home with. After I'd taken it, he ordered me a new coat, three pairs of shoes for various occasions, two shoulder bags and a purse. He let me enter the details from his bank card to complete the purchase, so I would feel confident enough to do it on my own the next time I *"needed"* to shop. Ha! As if that would ever happen.

I thanked Kolya so many times for his generosity. He put his hand over my mouth to stop me, then said, "Let me spoil you, Tess. It makes me happy to do so. Would you be so cruel and deny me happiness?"

What could I say to that?

20

TESS

Kolya spent the first two days with me after I left the hospital. The first day was about resting and getting familiar with the home that he told me was mine for however long I needed it. I wasn't sure how long that would be, and the thought of leaving really upset me, yet I knew it was inevitable.

The extended part of his home was huge, although it looked much smaller from the outside. My bedroom was next to Kolya's, followed by three further bedrooms and a study. There was also a spacious sitting room with a ridiculously large smart TV, a black leather sofa, and four reclining armchairs. At the other end of the room was a small bar area with a state-of-the-art stereo system.

Kolya informed me that the TV and stereo were linked to the best surround sound system he'd ever heard. I laughed and told him it was the only one I'd ever heard. To show how good it was, Kolya played some songs by U2—his favourite band. I recognised one song, "The Sweetest Thing," and smiled when Kolya sang it to me. Then he played "With or Without You" and took me in his arms, dancing with me while he sang, being careful of my arm and shoulder the whole time.

It was the first time I'd slow danced with anyone. I worried I'd step on his toes and giggled nervously, but then I got used to moving to the music with him.

I don't know what came over me, but I found myself pressing against him, holding on to his shoulders as tightly as I could. I felt strange, like I needed his warmth and energy or just…him. I'm not sure if it was the song that affected me, or dancing with him, but when it ended, I had tears in my eyes, though I didn't let them fall.

Kolya didn't ask me what was wrong when he looked down at me and noticed my tears. He just stared at me for a moment, as if he wanted to say something. But he must have thought better of it because he pulled away from me quickly, and then switched the music off.

After that, he took me on a tour around the rest of his home. There was the kitchen and utility room, which I was familiar with, and then we entered an area he told me was mainly for his staff.

I knew that Nate and Kevin lived in this part of the house; they shared a bedroom, a bathroom, and a sitting room. We didn't go into those areas as they weren't what Kolya had brought me to see. Instead, Kolya keyed a code into a room further down the hallway and led me into what looked like a NASA control room, only smaller. Kevin and another guy I hadn't met yet sat in front of computer screens. I noted a further sixteen screens of varying sizes, which not only showed different areas around the estate but also around the hotel Kolya had taken me to before he brought me here. Three of the screens displayed what appeared to be a castle.

Kolya informed me he'd bought Glengarran—an old Scottish castle—five years ago, so he could relax and go fishing. The castle had its own loch, and the grounds even contained a golf course. I thought the whole place looked beautiful and told him so. Half of it looked like a traditional manor house in places, but there were conical-shaped turrets placed randomly about the roof, which made it appear more like a castle. The façade boasted a huge oak door and reminded me of something I'd seen on TV. I liked old buildings and enjoyed learning the history behind them, so I asked quite a few questions about Glengarran.

Kolya promised he would take me as soon as he had the next few meetings out of the way. He said it was a place where you went to lose all your stress and worry, so he didn't want to take work with him.

Outside the extension was a twenty-five-metre swimming pool. Kolya said it was heated, though I could always use the one inside the sunroom if the weather was bad. That pool wasn't as large, but we could use it year-round because it was indoors—a significant benefit with the typically unpredictable British weather.

I loved swimming, although I hadn't been since I lived

with Jean. I remember having to go as a child at school, and I hated the swimsuits the pool staff loaned kids who couldn't afford or had forgotten their own. I'd moaned constantly to my mum about having to wear swimming costumes that were slightly too big and had gaping leg holes, so one day, she'd taken me shopping and stole one that I told her I liked.

I was mortified and was too scared to even try it on at first, but after another week of nearly exposing my girl parts in the way-too-big swimsuit the pool staff provided, I decided to wear it. It took two weeks for the feeling that the police would come and arrest me to pass, but when it did, I could get on with my swimming lessons without the fear of flashing anyone, and I learned to swim in record time.

The teacher said I was a natural and told me about a swimming team I could join on Saturdays. Like that would ever happen. If it cost anything to attend, I couldn't go. Every spare penny my mother had was spent on drugs. If it hadn't been for Mum getting housing benefits, we would have been homeless, and I often went days without food.

As I got older, I learned to always go with her when she collected her social security benefits. I'd take enough cash from her to feed us both and put the heating on in winter. If I didn't go, we went without—unless Mum stole something. She wasn't a very good thief. The drugs probably didn't help with that. Walking into supermarket displays because you're high doesn't help when you have a bag full of stolen milk, cheese, and eggs you're trying to keep hidden.

Kolya stood frowning at me while I told him all this. God, why did I have to tell him? I wasn't usually so chatty and open with people. Would he judge me? Would he ask Nan to lock away the valuables until I left?

"I'm not like my mum, Kolya. I don't steal. Your things will be safe with me, I promise."

"Tess, we are not our parents. Even if we have to walk the same path for a time, we don't have to tread in their exact footprints. We can make our own footprints and leap over the rocks and sticks that made them fall. My older brother Yuri has been made to walk my father's path, but so far, his steps haven't been so heavy. I pray that will never change. He hadn't wanted to take that road, but he wasn't given a choice."

"What is your father's business, Kolya? Is it similar to yours? You mentioned him before at the hospital. I remember you saying that's how you first became interested in weaponry."

"My father is a Bratva pakhan, which means he is a boss in the Russian mob. You see, *malyutka*, even though our financial circumstances were different, we both had a parent who broke the law to earn money. But I am willing to bet your mother hated what she did for money, whereas my father… Let's just say he's never lost sleep over the decisions he makes as a pakhan."

I was speechless! I mean, I'm not stupid—I know organised crime still happens. But other than the odd snippet in newspapers about the Kray twins from decades ago, there was little media coverage of modern mafia types here in Britain.

"Come, Tess, let us have a quick tour around the other building, then you can rest," Kolya suggested. "I have a meeting to prepare for later, so after we've eaten, I will retire to my office. Perhaps Danny and Bess will stop by and keep you company?"

The foyer of the manor house was impressive, the décor being Georgian in its appearance. With its exquisite wall and ceiling mouldings and simple yet elegant doorframes, it was a beautiful representation of the era. The walls were painted a pretty pastel yellow, which carried on up the long and winding staircase.

"Wow!" I exclaimed in what was almost a whisper as I took in the sheer elegance of the space.

"Kolya, how come you don't live here? Not that I don't like the extension, I mean."

"We did live here when Catherine was alive; it just never felt like home to us after she'd gone. So the extension I had built for my staff became a home for James and me. It makes more sense, anyway. Instead of a handful of staff in the extension and the rest dotted around the estate cottages, they can all live here. It's better for security."

"Do you think someone would attack your home?" I asked, unsure whether I wanted to hear his answer.

"One never knows the lengths someone will go to in gaining access to something they need. In my business, I cannot be too careful, as evidenced by what happened to you, Tess. That was the first time I'd ever let anyone else handle security, and most certainly the last. It will never happen again. The people I disappoint when I refuse their bids for my weaponry are many. I have to make sure both myself and my designs are protected."

He must have been able to see the nervousness and fear in my face because he added, "Do not worry, Tess. We fitted the extension with a unique state-of-the-art security system. If there is ever any threat, head straight inside and wait for Kevin and the team to do what they do best."

"Okay," I answered, doing well to hide the fear in my voice.

Kolya took me from the hallway into a large sitting room, which the beautiful marble fireplace should have dominated, but my eyes were drawn to a six-foot snooker table and bar area. There were large Chesterfield sofas and armchairs opposite a TV with at least a sixty-inch screen.

"Boss, Tess," Jonesy said, acknowledging our presence. He was watching a rugby match on the TV, which he paused before walking over to us.

"As you were, Jonesy. I haven't come in to ask you to work; I know it's your day off. I'm just showing Tess around so she's familiar with her new home."

"I don't mind showing you around, Tess. I gave Danny a tour after he was settled in his new room. I think he got a bit lost this morning when looking for the library, but little Bess remembered where the kitchen was, that's for sure. She's a clever one is Bess. She follows Ivan around because he's always eating, and he's taken to her like she's his own, soft as he is."

I loved Jonesy's singsong Welsh accent and friendly manner. Although he was tall—and by the size of his chest and arms, was very muscular—he wasn't at all intimidating. He had beautiful deep-blue eyes and an attractive, contagious smile. His nose was a little crooked, as if it had been broken at some point and not reset correctly. But it didn't detract from how handsome he was. He appeared to be a similar age to Kolya, and I wondered if he had a family.

"Is Danny with George or Devina?" Kolya asked.

Jonesy shook his head. "He came out about fifteen minutes ago. He said he felt tired and was going to get some sleep. You know what it's like after your first session. He'll be right as rain tonight."

"Well, if you see him later, let him know he's more than welcome to come over and visit Tess. I have to work, so I thought he could keep her company."

"Honestly, Kolya, I'm fine. I'm more than used to being on my own. I'll just read a book or something. Jonesy mentioned a library. I could find a book to read for later."

"We can stop at the library before we leave. I'm not sure there will be anything you would want to read in there, but you are more than welcome to browse. Now, let us leave Jonesy in peace to enjoy his day off. It's well deserved after the events of this week."

After saying goodbye to Jonesy, I asked about Danny and who George and Devina were. Kolya informed me that George and Devina were counsellors specialising in PTSD. He told me that all his employees were ex-military, apart from Nan and

Ivan, and all had seen active duty. Kolya said he believed it was important to keep his staff mentally and physically fit, so either George or Devina came and held weekly sessions with various staff.

Danny had told Kolya how severe his PTSD was, and he, in turn, had passed on whatever details they had spoken about to the counsellors. Kolya described Danny's first counselling session with the team as the first step in a long road to recovery. I hoped he was right. Danny deserved to be free of his demons.

"I will arrange for you to meet with them too, whenever you feel up to it," Kolya announced as we walked through the house.

I stopped and turned to look at him.

"Oh, no, I don't need to see anyone. I really am okay," I assured him. "There's nothing troubling me—other than the worry that Farid, Hassan, and Tariq might find me. And where Sarah might be."

"What about being shot? You may not think so now, but it could be something that causes you problems psychologically in the weeks and months to come. So it would be better that you speak with either George or Devina, whichever one you feel more comfortable with, sooner rather than later."

"No!" I told him firmly.

"What? Why?" he replied, shocked by my outright rejection.

"I don't want to sit and talk to a stranger about something that isn't bothering me. The only problem I have from being shot is the pain. And yeah, I was a little weepy at first, but I've endured much worse, so it won't break me."

Kolya stared at me for a few moments, making me slightly uncomfortable.

"You know, Tess, it might be a good idea to talk about what happened when you were attacked, and your life before that. It may help to share it with someone."

"I did. I told the social worker and the police, and that didn't do me any good. I shared it with Jean, Danny, and you, although maybe that wasn't such a good idea, considering you're trying to force me to admit it causes me problems that just aren't there."

"Tess, it was a traumatic event. It must cause you—"

"No, Kolya, it doesn't cause me anything. Anyway, who are you to tell me what I *must* feel? I thought you were an arms dealer, not a fucking psychologist," I yelled angrily.

"Do not swear at me, Tess. I am only trying to help, and it is not becoming of you."

I held his gaze for a moment, letting him see I wouldn't change my mind. It was a standoff I never wanted to have, and I wondered if my stubbornness and the minor argument would make him regret letting me stay here. My anger turned to anxiousness, then fear of being out there all alone again.

Kolya stepped towards me and held my face in his hands. He looked like he wanted to say something, but again, no words came.

"Please don't force me to see them, Kolya. I don't want anyone picking apart something that's in the past. It's done with, and I've moved on. I'm normally very guarded and find it hard to let people in, even if things bother me. Jean used to say I was one of life's copers. Give me a shit situation, and I'll cope with it the best way I can. That's just me. I'm happy with the way I am. So again, please don't force me to do something that could take away my strength and coping ability."

"I am sorry, *malyutka*. I will not ask you to go again. But you must promise me, if you ever feel you need to speak with them, you will let me know. I need you to understand that what the counsellors offer is nothing like you seem to imagine. You talk as though it makes you weak as a person to share your troubles. I ask you this, little one, do I seem weak to you?"

I shook my head, wondering where he was going with this.

"I was devastated when Catherine died. It ripped apart my heart, and my life became a shadow of what it once was. I felt lost and angry, too. Angry with Catherine for taking so many risks when out riding. But I had to be strong and pull myself together—be brave for my grieving son. I had to put aside my pain and grief to help James cope with the loss of his mother.

"I've always tried to be a good father, but my business took up a lot of my time, I am sorry to say, so Catherine had often taken on what should have been my parenting role. When she died, I tried to appear as if I was coping, but inside I was not. Then one evening, after James had gone to sleep, I came downstairs and happened to glance at some of the many photos Catherine had displayed on the walls. There was one of her and James with the horse she'd been riding when she'd fallen. I pulled it off the wall and threw it at the door. The glass shattered on impact, and the sound seemed to release something inside me. Something feral. I started pulling all the photos and pictures off the walls and throwing them at the door, walls, furniture—any hard surface that would make them smash. I didn't want to see her happy, smiling face when she had left me so miserable and alone.

"After I'd thrown the last one, Nan and Jack came to stand beside me. Nan asked me if throwing the photos had made me feel better. I thought it had while I was doing it. But when I saw the remnants of our happy family memories lying broken on the floor, I felt sick to my stomach. Nan took me in her arms and held me while I wept, and when I left, Jack and another member of my security team cleared all the broken bits of picture frame and glass away.

"Nan suggested I should see George so I could talk about the anger and grief running through me, and at first, I refused. But she told me I should lead by example. That if James could see I was able to speak about my grief, then he would, too. The woman knew what she was talking about regarding grief and suffering. She'd lost her only child after nursing him through years of ill health. So I did as Nan suggested and scheduled myself and James for a few sessions with George. In total, I had twenty sessions of grief counselling with him, and James had almost as many, too."

"Is that why there aren't many photographs of your wife here or in the other part of your home? Nan showed me a few of you and your son over there, but I've only seen one with your wife. She was very pretty."

"Yes, she was. She was modelling when we first met, but she turned her back on that when she became pregnant. She wanted to stay at home with James and be a full-time mum. Catherine had a nanny growing up, and although she loved her dearly, she'd said it was no substitute for having your parents around. Our family photos are now in the library and James's old playroom. I don't have many in the other part of the house. I'd felt guilty when I looked at them after the first time I…" Kolya looked away and shook his head. "Never mind. Let us forget about counselling for now. I need to take you to see the gym. Once the physiotherapist says it is okay, we will set you up with some gentle exercises to help build up the muscle tone in your arms and shoulders. The quicker we work on it, the more likely you will not suffer any long-term effects from your injury. Grayson said he was confident there had been no nerve damage, so you are very lucky in that respect. Just promise me you will never come to my rescue again, *malyutka*. I cannot stand to see you hurting."

After looking around the downstairs kitchen area, dining room, and another sitting room, Kolya showed me the sunroom that housed the indoor pool. Lucas had been swimming, and Kolya spoke to him regarding the next round of London meetings before we left. We then made our way to the gym, which was next door to the sunroom. Kolya informed me the room had been used as a ballroom many years ago, and when he opened the grand double doors, I could definitely see that.

The whole downstairs of the property had medium oak parquet flooring, but it was designed differently in this room. There was an inner rectangle of lighter oak with a single strip of black wood surrounding it, marking the area where everyone would have danced. But now, the sides of the room held various fitness equipment, including treadmills, rowing machines, and bikes. In the centre of the room was a boxing ring, where two men were fighting using some kind of martial arts. Franco was refereeing, but when he spotted us, he stopped the fight and came over.

"Boss." Franco nodded, acknowledging Kolya. Then he turned to me and said my name, his gaze boring into mine. For some reason, right at that moment, I felt intimidated by Franco. Not fearful, just… I don't really know or understand why, but his brown eyes held the kind of intensity that made me hyperaware of him.

"Franco, I was just telling Tess that once we get the go-ahead from the physiotherapist, we'll set her up with a gentle exercise program she can build upon. I will arrange for you and Jonesy to meet with them to discuss how best to implement those exercises with the equipment we have here. Tess tells me she likes to swim, so once the wound has healed enough, that could be the first step."

"I agree. Once we have her fighting fit, she could show us her moves in the ring. After all, by taking that bullet, Tess has proven she's one tough cookie."

"In the ring? Oh, no. I wouldn't be up for that...stuff," I told him, gesturing at the ring.

"Wouldn't you like to learn how to defend yourself against a would-be attacker?" Kolya asked.

"And wouldn't you like to be confident enough to fight back, even if it only helps you get away?" questioned Franco.

"Of course I would. But those guys were really going for it

in there, and they are about six feet of muscle. I'm only five foot four and have hardly any muscle at all. I would be no good against someone like them."

"You wouldn't be fighting, Tess. Just training, that's all. I'll make sure you're safe." Franco's words would have calmed my nerves a little, if he hadn't added, "Me and Jonesy are gonna make sure you're a crack shot, too. So you got all sides covered when it comes to protecting yourself."

"What? You mean shooting a gun? Like with real bullets? Why the hell would I need to learn how to shoot?"

"Weaponry is my business, Tess. And I think you'll enjoy the firing range. Women can be very competitive in there. Nan trained with Jonesy for ten weeks so she could beat Jack. She is exceptionally good with a rifle, although she does not seem as keen on handguns," Kolya said with a smile.

"Why don't you take her down and show her, boss? Maybe she won't look as scared once she's had a look around," Franco added while giving me an odd look. Like he was trying to get the measure of me. As if he knew I wouldn't want to go. And what was with the whole *"scared"* comment? I wasn't scared. Just bloody anxious I'd bitten off more than I could chew coming to live here—with all the counselling, fight-training, gun-firing bullshit they wanted to put me through. But then again, that seemed like a normal reaction for a seventeen-year-old girl who'd just been shot. And I didn't need to be qualified in psychology or counselling to determine that!

Kolya took my hand and began leading me out of the gym. I looked back to find Franco watching us. His eyes were fixed on our joined hands. It made me feel uncomfortable, so I tried to pull my hand away. But Kolya wouldn't let go, taking it as though I didn't want to see the firing range.

In truth, I was kind of curious. I imagined we would go outside to find targets on platforms or a similar setup to what the paintball ads depicted—with little shacks and wooden structures to hide behind. What I hadn't expected was for him to lead me to a doorway just inside the surprisingly modern kitchen, then down steep wooden steps into the cellar. When we got to the bottom, Kolya guided me towards a wooden shelving rack that housed numerous bottles of wine and spirits.

Kolya took out a bottle of port, five rows down and three rows in, then pulled out what appeared to be a small smartphone attached to a wire. He held his thumb over it for a few seconds before something clicked. The wine rack began sliding to the left, a doorway appearing in its place. He then keyed a series of numbers into a keypad attached to the thick steel door before it opened. As we stepped inside, he flicked several switches, lighting up a room that looked a little like I'd seen on American cop shows.

There were four firing lanes on each side of the room, with a door to the far wall. Behind the door, a small room housed twenty-five steel gun cabinets, which were locked by iris scanners. I watched silently while Kolya stared into a scanner until a red beam moved along the device, and the cabinet opened.

"How come you have all this technology locking the guns away? Surely the fingerprint scan thing was enough?" I asked, curious as to why he would go to these lengths.

"There are weapons in here that one cannot obtain licences

for in the UK. Handguns, of course, but you can own some semi-automatic rifles if you have the correct licence."

Kolya removed a large black rifle with a scope at the top, which he took a few moments to adjust. Then he reached into the cabinet and brought out a box of ammunition, explaining how to load the bullets into the magazine. He showed me how to make the gun safe and then walked to the first firing lane, handing me a set of ear defenders from a rack by the door before loading the magazine into the rifle.

There was a male silhouette target on a white card, like on those TV cop shows, which made this whole experience seem unreal. After showing me how to aim, Kolya slipped two small earplugs into his ears, removed the safety from the rifle, and proceeded to fire five shots at the target.

I flinched a little when he fired the first shot, but the rest didn't bother me at all. It didn't sound anything like the shot that hit me less than a week ago, but I wasn't wearing ear defenders then, and this was an entirely different gun.

After the last shot was fired, Kolya made the rifle safe and ejected the magazine before lowering it onto the countertop in front of him. He pressed a button on the outside of the cage-like wire that framed each lane and brought the target towards us. All the bullets had hit the target in the centre, where the silhouette pointed a gun from his midsection. This confused me, as I always thought you aimed for the head. In almost all TV shows, the bad guys end up with a hole in the centre of their forehead or their chest. Kolya told me you were less likely to miss if you aimed for the midsection, which is obviously larger than the head.

"If they move slightly, you are still likely to get a shot in," he said. That made sense, and bizarrely, for someone who had just been shot and had zero interest in guns before, I found the whole thing fascinating.

The room was quite cold, and I shivered a little. Kolya noticed and apologised for the temperature. He told me it was the ventilation system that made it so cool. It was there to remove contaminants from the bullets and any smoke that may arise. It also had to keep the building at negative air pressure. Kolya gave me loads of scientific information regarding this, which I barely took in as it was way above my head.

I shivered again and began to feel strange—like I was looking at Kolya through a glass that distorted his image. Within seconds I felt all right again, but Kolya had noticed and became concerned. He took out his phone and called Nate to come and lock the gun away, then apologised for disturbing him. He said he should have known it was too soon to take me exploring the property like this.

He put his arm around me and guided me out of the firing range towards the steep wooden steps of the cellar, telling me to take it slowly as we climbed them.

Once we were back in the kitchen, he pulled out a chair and crouched down in front of me until he was sure I wouldn't pass out. I told him he was fussing for nothing, and I was perfectly fine now, which was true. But Kolya was having none of it.

He took a tall glass from a cupboard and walked over to a large, fully stocked refrigerator. After pouring me a glass of orange juice and commanding I drink it, Kolya went back to the cellar to lock the doors until Nate got there. He said they never left guns out of their cabinets or the cellar unlocked, reminding me again that some of its contents weren't exactly legal. He told me they never speak about it outside his property, so if anyone asked, I should deny all knowledge of it.

I wondered, at that moment, why he'd let me see it. For him to do so showed a level of trust that both surprised and flattered me in equal measure. He wasn't treating me like some poor, misguided teenager. He was treating me as an adult —something I appreciated more than he could ever know.

21

TESS

I love my Kindle! The little device Kolya bought me eased the boredom while he demanded I rest. After nearly passing out during our trip to the gun range, he forbade me from venturing any further than the part of the property we lived in.

Danny and Bess had been coming over to visit every day, which I was so grateful for. It helped relieve some of the boredom my confinement created. I know it helped Danny, too. He was loving it here. Being part of a *"unit,"* as he called it, felt familiar to him, even if the people in his *unit* weren't. He'd also had two visits with Devina, the counsellor. Danny said they were more exhausting than the workouts Franco created for him.

He was due to start helping Jack out around the grounds of the property over the next few days. He told me he was ready for it. Danny said having a purpose in life felt like another step on the road to recovery, and just now, the handyman/gardener's job was his purpose.

It got me thinking… What was my purpose?

For the moment, I had to remain hidden. No one had come looking for me yet. There were no news reports about two missing teenagers from South Yorkshire regarding Sarah and I —other than on the local police Facebook page. Kevin had been monitoring all avenues of media.

The only person who'd miss us in any way was Jean. Kolya allowed me to speak to her via the burner phone he'd sent her. She'd been so worried about me and wanted to come and see for herself that I was okay.

We talked about Sarah a lot, both of us desperate for information. The police had paid Jean three visits about the two of us—asking her if she'd heard from us or if she had any idea where we might be. Beth had told the police we'd gone to live with our boyfriends. Of course, Sarah had run away numerous times before, so I think they weren't overly concerned at first. She'd always come home within a day or two. But this time, it was different, so why weren't they doing more to find her? Did not having a family to care for you mean your life was less important?

I knew Kolya had a long conversation with Jean the day I came out of the hospital. He'd reassured her he was looking after me and would keep me safe. He also said he would arrange for her to come and visit—something I was looking forward to more than anything.

I never thought I would say this, but I was really missing school. I should have been preparing for the exams I'd studied so hard for, but it looked unlikely I'd be going back to my school at this point. Kolya told me he would try to arrange something with the education authority when it was safe for me to reveal where I was. But when would that be? All Kolya ever said about the Tariq, Hassan, and Farid situation was that he was taking care of it, but it would take time. He said I should forget about everything and concentrate on getting better.

I wasn't feeling ill or weak anymore—just a little sore. Something to be expected after being shot ten days ago. Over the last couple of days, moving my arm and shoulder had become easier. Layla, the physiotherapist Kolya hired, had given me what she called *"exercises"* to do in order to prevent my muscles from becoming stiff. They weren't really exercises, just repetitive, everyday movements. Within the last day or so, I'd been able to stop taking painkillers throughout the day. But to my dismay, I'd had to take them again last night. I'd fallen asleep reading a new vampire series on my Kindle and had slept awkwardly. I'd woken up at 4 a.m. with a throbbing pain throughout my shoulder and upper back, so it was my own fault, and as I found my Kindle hard to put down, I needed to find a more comfortable way to read at night. There was no way I was giving up reading in bed or anywhere else for that matter.

Reading provided me with an escape from reality I so desperately needed. One where I didn't have to think about what Sarah's disappearance might mean. One where I wasn't recovering from a gunshot wound, unable to go back to the life I lived before. Not that I'd want to. My life here with

Kolya and his staff differed completely from either my time at The Willows or with my mum. I wanted for nothing. Anything I expressed an interest in became mine. Hence the Kindle. Accompanying that were an iPad and MacBook. Now those I hadn't even mentioned in passing, but I loved them all the same.

I'd never had my own tablet or laptop before. We used computers at school, and there were two at The Willows, although one never worked, and the lads hogged the other one.

Jean had a laptop she let us use any time we wanted. She only had it for ordering her shopping and paying bills online, so it was nearly always free. But to have one of my very own was like I'd come up in the world. No longer was I Tess, the poor foster kid; I was Tess, the spoiled little princess. And all it had taken was a bullet to the shoulder… Yep, my thoughts went down that dark, sarcastic route sometimes. A defence mechanism, I think, in case one day it was all taken away from me.

I couldn't log in to my Hotmail account; Kevin said someone might trace it. So I mostly spent my time online Googling random stuff and watching YouTube videos with Ivan and Jonesy. They both loved to watch those gross yet strangely satisfying pimple-popping videos, or those with people making ill-timed leaps onto Tarzan swings and other stupid, wholly avoidable accidents. Both Ivan and Jonesy together were like a comedy duo and often had me howling with laughter at their antics.

Ivan had brought me flowers and chocolate every day since I arrived at Kolya's home. Granted, he always ate more of the chocolate than I did, but the thought was there. The flowers were wild ones he'd picked on his daily morning walk with Danny and Bess, and I'd gone with them for the past three days.

The grounds of Kolya's home were so pretty. There were one hundred acres of well-kept lawns and woodland. The prettiest place of all was the wildflower meadow. The day we walked to that, I spotted two different types of butterflies and three rabbits.

We were now in the month of May, and the weather was unusually hot for this time of the year. As per what usually happens when any part of my body sees the sun, my freckles became more apparent. I'd had a slight sunburn, too, so Nan gave me some of her sun creams until the high SPF ones Kolya ordered for me arrived.

I hate my colouring. I'd always wanted the type of complexion you see on the models in magazines. But I could never achieve that perfectly flawless look because of my ever-increasing freckles.

Nan said she loved my colouring, as did Kolya, but they weren't the ones stuck with it. I could have rocked the Celtic look if I had blue or green eyes.

At times, my eye colour almost appears amber. Kolya told me they were stunningly beautiful, but it was his eyes that were beautiful. I could stare into them all day long and never tire of doing so. I often had to stop myself from looking at him. There wasn't anything about his appearance I didn't like.

The first time I saw him coming out of the gym wearing just his workout shorts—shirtless and covered with a light sheen of sweat—I stood there open-mouthed, unable to move. I felt warm all over and had a powerful compulsion to reach out and touch him. To place my hand on his chest or the abs that tapered down to the waistband of his shorts. My mouth became dry, and I was sure he'd be able to hear how fast and loud my heart was beating.

He leaned in to kiss me on the cheek as he passed by me, and that slight touch was enough to have me growing hot and wet between my legs. I was so embarrassed by my body's reaction that I tried to avoid Kolya for a few days. Of course, he wasn't having any of it. Other than working out, he spent as much of his free time with me as he could.

We watched movies together, talked about literature, current affairs, Ivan's obsession with pizza and all things sugary—anything, really. Not once did he treat me like a child.

I suppose my experiences over the years had ripped any semblance of a normal childhood away from me. From the years spent caring for my drug-addicted mother to the reason why I ended up in foster care. I couldn't remember ever really feeling like a child. Jonesy and Ivan treated me like their little sister, and Nan babied me like she did all the guys who worked for Kolya.

I considered Nate and Kevin friends. I knew they shared a bedroom, but I wasn't aware of their relationship until I caught them in a passionate kiss outside the tech room. I was so shocked I just stood there, staring. I mean, the only gay men I'd ever seen before were the camp characters in TV shows, and there was one lad at school who was more effeminate than the girls he hung around with. So to me, with my limited, naïve experience of the world outside of Doncaster, it didn't seem possible that men as musclebound and tough as Nate and Kevin could be gay.

They told me they'd been together as a couple for the last four years—eight weeks after Nate came to work for Kolya. Kevin had been running Kolya's technical security for a year before Nate arrived. I loved that no one judged them for being gay, but Nate said it hadn't always been the case. One of Kolya's guards had been so outraged he'd attacked Kevin one evening. Although Kevin was quite capable of defending himself, the other guy caught him by surprise, and when Kevin's head hit the floor, it knocked him unconscious. Nate said if it hadn't been for Franco stumbling upon the attack, Kevin would have ended up with a much longer hospital stay than a night in A&E.

Franco had beaten the other guy bloody, and when Kolya found out what the homophobic prick had done, he terminated his employment with immediate effect.

Nate said he'd known Franco for many years, having served in the army with him before they both came to work for Kolya. But since the night he'd saved Kevin, he'd become like a brother, and one of the best friends he'd ever had.

It made me see Franco in a different light. From the few times I'd been in his presence, I hadn't known what to make of him. Something in his big brown eyes let you know he'd seen enough of the evil in this world to make him indifferent to it, but that didn't seem the case with him. Franco cared about his friends and the things he believed in. Although he was a man of few words, those words were always effective whenever he spoke.

Every evening he came to check I'd done the exercises that the physiotherapist had given me, even though they seemed pointless. He even gave me a few extra to do—which I protested at. But he goaded me into doing them after insinuating I was getting too used to being a pampered female.

After I'd finished my exercises, Franco took off his T-shirt, revealing a scar from a bullet wound in exactly the same place as mine. I'd been dumbstruck. Without thinking, I reached out and touched it, tracing the outside of the distorted circular scar with my index finger. He'd hitched in a breath, and for a moment, I thought I'd hurt him. I apologised profusely and pulled my hand away. Franco grabbed my wrist and brought my fingers back to the puckered skin, telling me as he did so that mine would look much better when it healed, and that I shouldn't be afraid of an external scar because the event that caused it was over and done with. He said the wound you couldn't see was another matter, and I could certainly do something about that.

Franco told me to get my shit together, push through my strengthening exercises, and then go see George or Devina. When I opened my mouth to protest, he held up his hand and told me he didn't want to hear what he called my *"whiny-ass excuses."* Then he turned and walked away before I could toss back a reply, slipping his T-shirt on as he went. But not before I'd seen the back of his shoulder and the scar left behind by the bullet's exit wound.

22

KOLYA

The exuberant atmosphere in my home today affected all my staff. Even the little dog, Bess, was more excitable than usual.

Nan had been planning for James's arrival for the last two weeks, and she'd covered my home in both *welcome home* and *happy birthday* banners. Tess had joined her in the kitchen many times over the last few days, baking my son's favourite party foods. James turned twenty years old today, but Nan still thought of him as the child she'd taken care of for so many years.

I miss him every single day, and so often wished I'd dug my heels in and insisted he studied here in the UK. My father wanted him to study in Moscow, but that could never happen. It was hard enough to secure his safety here and in the US. I doubt Russia would ever be a haven for my only son and heir.

Today will be the first time James has met Tess face-to-face. He insisted on speaking to her during our video call when I first brought her home, wanting to meet the person who saved my life—to thank her himself for doing so. At first, she seemed uncomfortable, which was probably because James wouldn't stop calling her his hero. But over the last few weeks, they'd built up a friendship, of sorts.

James tells her all about his studies; how living in the States compares with living in the UK, and Tess lets him know all that's going on around here. Brad—James's best friend and housemate—usually joins in on their video calls, and I've often heard both Tess and Nan laughing over his antics. Brad will join him on this trip. His father manages KOLCAT Engineering in the US, and both James and Brad will work alongside him as soon as they complete their studies.

My staff will also celebrate the return of James's guards, Carl and Tanner. James has a security team of five who rotate guarding him in shifts.

Carl and Tanner, who are both former marines, came to work for me when James was fourteen; they've been part of his close protection team ever since. I trust them implicitly with my son's safety, but I was looking forward to speaking with them in person regarding how we should progress with James's security. Especially now that he's socialising more. I worry about him getting stoned or drunk at wild parties—like I did when I was his age.

My father, my business, and James's own personal worth because of my father-in-law's legacy could make my son a target.

I often thought how it would be if we were a normal family, without everything that compromised our safety.

Jonesy told me I'd have worries just the same, like paying for James's university tuition, him learning to drive and buying a car, who he was hanging around with, or him getting a girl pregnant.

Better any of those than the threat of him being kidnapped and held for ransom.

Hearing a squeal of laughter, I looked out the window of my study over to the basketball court to find Tess sitting on Ivan's shoulders, trying to secure a *Happy Birthday* banner onto the board behind the hoop.

Opening the window, I called out for Tess to get down, but she couldn't hear me over the songs from the music system Franco was testing out. Leaving the study, I ran into Nan. She was holding a tray of sandwiches in one hand and a jug of lemonade in the other.

"Oh, there you are, Kolya. Do me a favour and take this outside. We need to keep Ivan full and away from the food in here."

"Have you seen what he and Tess are doing?" I asked, ignoring her request.

"Yes. They're fixing banners to the backboards of the basketball hoops. I know you'll all end up on the court at some point, so I thought it would be a nice surprise."

"But she's sat on his shoulders, Nan. If she falls from that height, God only knows what could happen to her. It was only last week the physiotherapist stopped coming. She shouldn't be taking risks like that."

I turned to leave again, but Nan's words stopped me in my tracks.

"Kolya, she's not Catherine. Tess won't chase the rush like Catherine did. She's not like that. Tess is cautious, steady, and happy with the life she's living now. Catherine lived a different life before she met you. She wasn't used to hearing no. From what she told me, her father gave in to her every whim. By her own admission, Catherine lived life to the extreme when she was single. Bungee jumping off bridges in five different countries, deep sea diving around sharks with just a cage for protection, riding her horse without proper headgear. She needed the thrill—a boundary to push against. She had a *live for today* attitude, despite knowing she had to be there for her husband and son. Tess is different. She doesn't crave a rush that could risk her tomorrows. She loves it here with the family she's become part of and the safety she feels. Don't put limits on her happy times just because you feel anxious."

"But Ivan is so tall! He should know better than to—"

"Kolya, do you *really* think Ivan would risk doing something that could put her in danger? He adores Tess. We all do. She's brought a breath of fresh air to this family. She's like the daughter I never had. Hearing her laugh, seeing her smile… it warms my heart. Let's enjoy that, Kolya. It's been a long time coming."

Nan handed me the sandwiches and lemonade before grabbing some glasses and ushering me outside.

"Kolya," Tess yelled when she spotted me. I placed the sandwiches and lemonade on the glass patio table and walked over to the basketball court. After Tess had secured the last banner, Ivan lowered to his knees so I could lift her off his shoulders. I held her in my arms for a moment, enjoying the innocence and beauty of her smiling face.

"You've caught the sun, my darling. I see more of those pretty freckles appearing across your nose," I told her, peppering tiny kisses across it as she groaned.

"I'm wearing SPF fifty, and I've been out here less than twenty minutes. If you covered me in a sheet, I'd still come out in bloody freckles."

Tess huffed out a heavy sigh that lifted copper-coloured curls away from her eyes. Her growing number of freckles was something she detested, yet I found adorable.

Her natural beauty captivated me. More so every day. In the ten weeks I'd known her, she'd changed from a girl to a woman. Tess had put on weight she so desperately needed, gaining curves I shouldn't have noticed yet couldn't stop thinking about. She gained strength and muscle tone with the swimming and workouts she did with Jonesy and Franco almost every day. No longer did I call her *malyutka* or little one. The endearment didn't fit her anymore.

Tess had grown into a strong, confident young woman, ready to take on the world. But I worried that wouldn't last once the letter and recording from Farid Ali were in the hands of the police.

I'd discussed it with my security team two weeks ago and planned to send it to the police within the next two days. Then James informed me he'd be through with classes early, so he could come home for his birthday. I didn't want Tess's first meeting with my son to be shrouded with worry and sadness, but when she learned the circumstances behind the death of her friend, I knew she'd be utterly distraught. So I kept the letter and recording here in my safe.

Tess knew we'd apprehended Farid Ali at my hotel. I told her we'd handed him over to the police and left it at that. Obviously, there'd been nothing on the news channels about his arrest. Tess assumed it was because they were gathering evidence against him, which she understood would take time. I worried I'd lose her trust when I had to tell her the truth. Yet, despite that worry, I did not regret my actions. The man deserved to die; there was no doubt of that in my mind. The question was, would Tess keep that secret and remain here with me?

23

TESS

James and Brad were a laugh a minute. Both were getting drunk at James's birthday party, although they blamed jet lag and not the alcohol they were consuming.

Kolya looked so happy to have James at home, and the party seemed like it would continue well into the night.

James invited me to join him in the video call he was making to his grandfather. I'd seen photographs of a much younger Roman Barinov, but to see him on the screen in the same room as Kolya and James was really something else.

The younger Barinov men were more or less the image of Roman, albeit without the grey hair and lines around their eyes. But he'd definitely aged well and looked much younger than his sixty-eight years. He smiled warmly when James introduced me, then told me in English that he'd been waiting to speak to me so he could thank me for saving his son. He said he was forever in my debt and would grant me anything I wished. I told him that wasn't necessary; Kolya was making sure I had everything I could ever need. But then he said the strangest thing. Looking at Kolya, he told him he should keep me within the family. That I would be a good wife who could bear him another child.

Kolya admonished Roman, reminding him of my age, to which he shrugged as if it meant nothing. Then, turning to James, he asked if *he* would like to wed me. James laughed it off, protesting that we'd only just met and were way too young to settle down. Roman replied, "Age is just a number, James, and when you find a woman who is meant for our way of life, you give her our name, and you never let her go." He then pointed at me, saying, "You, my dear, will bear the name Barinov. Of this, I am sure."

Kolya led me from the room after the video call had ended, apologising for his father's words. Strangely enough, what Roman said hadn't upset me, though Kolya's instant dismissal of me because of my age left me feeling a little deflated. So I excused myself for an hour and paid Danny and Bess a visit. A fuss from that sweet little dog and a hug from Danny never failed to lift my spirits.

What I wanted to do after that was disappear to my room and lose myself in one of the many romance books I'd downloaded on my Kindle. One where the hero charges after the woman he loves and tells her she's his, then makes love to her all night long. God, if I had a pound for every time I'd imagined Kolya doing that to me over the last month or so, I'd be rolling in money.

I know that realistically, Kolya's right. I'm so much

younger than him, and my lack of experience would most likely bore him. Plus, I've seen photos of his late wife and there's no way I could compare to her.

Catherine was stunning. Tall with long, pale blonde hair, big blue eyes and beautiful skin that seemed to glow from within. The complete opposite of me: short and freckle faced with mad curly, copper-coloured hair, and dark amber eyes that looked like they belonged more on a wolf than a human.

At first, I thought I was falling for Kolya because of the situation we found ourselves in: me saving his life, then him taking care of me. But over the last few weeks, I've enjoyed every moment I've spent with him, and I love the way he shows his affection.

If we're going for a walk around the grounds, he often holds my hand. He always hugs me when he comes back home from business meetings and, actually, he hugs me a lot. But then again, so do Nan and Nate. Ivan, too.

I'd never invited hugs or any kind of physical affection before. Not even from my mum or Jean. Sarah hugged me and I was okay with that. But receiving hugs from Kolya and his staff seemed so natural now.

Kolya also likes to give me little butterfly kisses on my cheek or my forehead, and strangely enough, my fingers. I've often wondered what he'd do if, when he was kissing my cheek, I turned my face so that my lips met his. I've imagined how they would feel against my own and if…

No! I had to stop torturing myself, because that's exactly how it feels to know what you want more than anything can never happen.

If I turned my face so our lips could meet, my life here would change. He might ask me to leave—something I just didn't want.

I felt like part of the family here, with Kolya, Nan, and these tough yet sweet men. I would miss them so much if I left. Even Franco and his slave-driving workouts I bitch about. I know he does it for my own good, and I've seen the way he looks at me when I've hit one of his targets. Like he's proud of me and how far I've come after being shot. He's easy on the eyes, too, and if I wasn't already head over heels for Kolya, I could *really* crush on him.

"Hey, Tess, where are you?" I heard Brad yell, bringing me out of my thoughts about my life here and the people in it. He was in the kitchen, eating some of the delicious birthday cake Nan made for James.

"I can't believe you're still hungry," I told him when he grabbed another slice. I swear today I'd seen him eat as much as Ivan. Both Brad and James were around six feet in height and were already quite muscular in an athletic sort of way.

"What? I'm a growing boy. Well, that's what Nan says, so I'm going with that. Where've you been, anyway? James and Kolya are video calling his godfather. We thought he was flying in tomorrow, but he says he has a business emergency and can't leave Greece until it's resolved. We're spending a few days with him before we fly home. Have you ever been to his island, Tess?"

"No, I've not. I haven't been able to get a passport yet."

I'd spoken to Yannis Markos three times when he'd video called Kolya. He's one of Kolya's best friends, and it was his guards that should have been protecting him and Kolya the day I was shot.

Yannis had just gone through a complicated and messy divorce. Kolya said it was the third time he'd been married, so he should have known how to make it work by now. He also told me Yannis's first wife left him for his father. Some screwed-up family values there, that's for sure. He never got the chance to divorce that wife. Both she and his father died after there was a freak explosion on their yacht. A tragic experience all round for Yannis.

Kolya said it changed him and his attitude towards women after that, and he'd since married two complete divas who were nothing but gold diggers. Luckily, being the only son of a Greek shipping tycoon, he was able to pay them off and be done with them. Though I can't imagine how easy it would be to do so. I mean, surely he would have loved them once or he wouldn't have married them. Kolya said there are many people who marry for reasons other than love. I couldn't do that. Love would be the *only* reason I would marry someone.

"Kolya has two private jets and two helicopters. I'm sure he could sneak you out of the country somehow, Tess. You could come to Greece with us. Or, if you want to wait for your passport, come back to the US with us when we leave. You'd have to get a visa, but—"

"I can't, Brad. Not until I'm eighteen. I'm a ward of the court, which means the state makes all my legal decisions. I'm not allowed to apply for a passport in my own right until I'm eighteen, and who knows where I'll be by then. I don't have a job or money of my own, and I don't know how long Kolya will want me here," I told him.

"You're not going anywhere, Tess. Trust me on that. And you'll never need to worry about money, either. Not with Kolya looking out for you. But it's always good to have choices or options in life. It's important you remember that."

With that last comment, Brad left the kitchen, touching my shoulder on his way out.

Choices? Options? Yes, people like Brad and James do have options. They have wealthy fathers who make sure they want for nothing; trust funds for when they finish their degrees —which they don't have to work two jobs to pay for—and employment to walk into when they complete their education.

From what I remember of having choices, they weren't *all that*. Choosing whether I ate or kept the house warm and electricity on so I could stay up and do my homework was always a tough one.

The only choice *I'd* made while being here was not to see the counsellors, and both Kolya and Franco had let me know they weren't happy about that. So at the moment, I'd prefer not to have choices or options thank you very much!

24

KOLYA

With a headache to rival any other, I was grateful for the tinted windows on my helicopter, yet I still needed the shade of my sunglasses. I had no one else to blame but myself, of course. Staying up until the early hours, drinking and playing poker with James, Brad, Franco, Jonesy, and Kevin. Though why the hell we'd bothered to take on Kevin at poker was beyond me. It may have been the alcohol that made us brave, but it was no excuse. We all knew we'd leave the table with our pockets so much lighter, yet we did it anyway.

I enjoyed the distraction, despite losing so spectacularly, and I was happy to see Brad join us because it kept him away from Tess. I was becoming increasingly irritated by the attention he showered her with. I know he's a flirt, and I have no issues with whom he uses his charms on when he's back home in the States. But Tess is out of bounds.

He'd annoyed me so much yesterday, and I was about to say something, but then I overheard James telling him to leave Tess well alone. He'd said she felt like a sister to him, in a weird sort of way, so he couldn't deal with him hitting on her like he did with the girls on campus. Brad denied doing anything other than being friendly with Tess, to which James laughed, then said, "Yeah, right. Tell me another, I might believe that one."

I am hoping Brad takes the hint and keeps his distance until they fly to Greece to stay with Yannis. In the meantime, I have arranged for Franco to increase Tess's training at the range. Now that her strength has increased, she's able to hold the rifle steady and has proved an excellent shot. She doesn't seem bothered by any of the guns, which could have been the case given her recent experience.

Tess still refuses to see George or Devina for counselling. She became so angry and upset with me when I suggested it, and I didn't want a repeat of that. At some point in the future, the traumatic events of her life might come back to haunt her. But forcing her to confront them when she wasn't ready to do so wouldn't help her, either.

As we came in to land, I saw Tess, James, and Brad around the outdoor pool. The weather had been much warmer than usual over the last few weeks, and we'd all made use of the outdoor areas.

Nan had given over some of the cooking to Tanner, who made the tastiest marinade to coat all the meat he regularly barbecued. He was territorial over the whole thing and wouldn't let anyone near until the steaks were cooked to perfection. My stomach growled just thinking about them, so I hoped it wouldn't be too long until we sat down to eat.

After dropping my briefcase in the kitchen, I grabbed a glass of orange juice and a couple of painkillers for the headache, then made my way to the pool area, delighting in the sound of Tess's unbridled laughter. The sight that greeted me when I got there, however, made me see red. Brad stood behind Tess, his chest pressed firmly against her back, his arms around her waist so she couldn't escape. He yelled, "You're going in," before lifting her off the side of the pool and launching them both into the water.

I stalked towards the pool, reaching the edge just as Tess surfaced, spluttering and wiping the water from her eyes.

"I can't believe you did that, Brad. You're a pest. Just you wait. I'll get you when you least expect it, and I'll make it bloody count," she shouted, swimming over to the side of the pool when she noticed me.

Brad remained in the deep end, laughing, which was probably a good thing.

If he climbed out, I would most likely punch him.

"Are you okay?" I asked, helping Tess out of the pool.

"Yes, I'm fine. He won't be once I'm finished with him, though. And your son. Nothing but pests, both of them."

"Why are you including me? I didn't throw you in *this time*," James replied, finally looking up from his book. "Hey, Dad, how's the hangover?"

"Hanging on," I told him, glancing at the book he was reading. It was one I'd almost memorised in my youth about the progression and changes in weaponry over the last century, and how those changes influenced the various wars they were used in.

I'd told my son on many occasions that we cannot create better weapons for the future without learning about those from the past. Right now, it appeared as if he'd been listening, which is never a bad thing for a parent to see. I've often wondered if James had a genuine interest in KOLCAT beyond it being the family business. I would hate to think he was doing it just to please me.

"Toss her back in, Kolya; she needs cooling down," Brad yelled, inciting my anger once again as I recalled how close he had been to her near-naked body before jumping into the water.

I pulled Tess towards me, holding her wet body against mine. She was wearing a one-piece swimsuit that hid the scar from her bullet wound. I was glad about that. Seeing it always had me on edge, reminding me of the day I held her in my arms as she cried out in pain and fear, her blood soaking my clothes as her wet hair and swimsuit did now.

Brad swam to the side of the pool and climbed out. At first, it appeared as though he was heading to one of the sun loungers, but he quickly spun back towards Tess, who had stepped away from me to grab a towel. I intervened immediately, taking hold of the hand that Brad reached out to grab Tess with, and in a move my security would be proud of, had

Brad up and over my shoulder, tossing him head-first into the pool before he had the chance to protest.

"Dad, what the fuck was that?" James questioned with a grin.

"Payback," I replied, then added, "James, try not to swear in front of Tess; it's a habit she is trying to break."

"You are my hero," Tess declared, smiling as she leapt into my arms.

"Whoa! You nearly had us both in the water then. Is that what you want, my darling? Do you miss the pool so much that you want to get back in?" I teased, moving nearer to the edge.

"You wouldn't," she stated, her bare legs wrapping around my waist as her arms tightened around my neck. I placed one hand under her bottom to keep her in place, then stepped back towards her sun lounger and emptied my pockets. She shook her head; her copper curls seemed two shades darker when wet. Still holding her in my arms, I kicked off my shoes and stepped back towards the edge of the pool. She was laughing now, her mouth resting against my neck, the sound sending vibrations across my skin.

We had an audience. My son, Brad, and at least four members of my staff. Yet the moment seemed so intimate. Every feminine part of her was pressed against me, and I felt a familiar stirring in my boxers as my cock hardened. I needed to get us in the pool before anyone noticed.

For one more precious moment, I held her body tight against mine, then I kissed her cheek and asked, "Are you ready for this, Tess?"

She lifted her head, looked into my eyes and said, "More than you'll ever know."

I wanted to gaze upon her face while I asked her to clarify the words she'd just uttered with such a serious expression, but if I waited any longer, no one would fail to notice the erection straining against the fabric of my clothing. As it was, I had to lift Tess higher as I took the last step to the edge of the swimming pool. I couldn't let her feel my desire for her.

While my body was more than ready to show Tess how I felt, my mind was not. So, after one more second of what felt like utter bliss, I took that last step into the pool.

25

KOLYA

I came up from under the water mere seconds after Tess and was pleased to note she was laughing while attempting to swim away. I swam towards her, grabbing her around the waist as she reached the side of the pool. I knew I shouldn't be doing this, but I couldn't help myself. Seeing Brad touching her was like a red rag to a bull. It was all kinds of wrong to be so angry and possessive. Blame it on the headache or the exhilarating feeling of jumping into the water fully clothed, but at this very second, I just didn't care.

I put my arms on either side of her head, caging her in, the water lapping gently around us. My infatuation with this beautiful girl, my saviour in so many ways, had reduced me to this: a man who should know better than to be led by sexual need.

Tess grabbed my shirt, stating, "Your clothes are wet!"

I traced my fingers along the strap of her swimsuit. "What a coincidence. So are yours."

She smiled, nervously at first, but then it turned slightly wicked. I returned her smile, my erection pulsing back to life when I leaned in closer.

"Boss."

"What is it?" I snapped.

I looked up to find Jonesy staring down at me; the expression on his face was grim.

"Kevin needs to speak with you immediately. There's been a development." I watched his eyes move from me to Tess, then back again.

I didn't ask if it could wait; Kevin wasn't one for unnecessary drama. Though it pained me to do so, I hauled myself from the pool, leaving Tess with just a kiss on her cheek.

It was just as well we were interrupted. If it wasn't for Jonesy, I would have kissed the mouth I found so tempting, pressed against the body I had no right to covet. What was I thinking? My son had been watching, along with Brad.

As soon as I thought of him, I knew why I'd been prepared to cross those boundaries with Tess.

I was jealous.

On paper, he would be the right man for her. Just two years older. Smart. Wealthy. Able to support her. Probably liked the same music, movies, and whatever else would interest someone of their age. They would have more things in common than she'd ever have with me. He was competition; simple as that.

I shouldn't even want Tess that way.

I was nearly twenty-three years older, more set in my ways. Yes, I could provide her with anything money can buy, protect her, worship the ground she walks on and love her more than life itself. But would that be enough when she could find the same with a much younger man? And more to the point, would Tess want that? Or did she envisage something else in her future?

After stripping out of my wet shirt and trousers, I threw them over one of the poolside chairs, glad I no longer had the hard-on I'd been sporting. Following Jonesy inside, I told him to let Kevin know I'd be five minutes.

My bedroom overlooked the pool, and with the window open, I heard James tell Brad he was coming in to see what was wrong. I walked to the window and looked out. No matter the emergency, I didn't want to leave Tess out there on her own with Brad. To my relief, I saw her heading towards the house with James, a towel wrapped around her body.

I felt myself breathe a little easier, and yet… Fuck! I had to stop with this unhealthy obsession. I needed to get my head together to deal with whatever development had emerged.

I dropped my wet boxers in the laundry basket in my bathroom and then threw on my gym shorts and a T-shirt. After I'd spoken to Kevin, perhaps a workout would help? Something to get my blood pumping—somewhere other than my groin.

Kevin was busy in the tech room, where he monitors all my security. On one of the larger screens, I could see a news channel, which was currently on pause.

I took a seat and waited until he finished a telephone conversation with Rashid before I spoke to him.

"Kevin, Jonesy informed me of a development you needed to speak to me about. What is it?"

"Jonesy and Nate have already seen this, and I'm just waiting for a few of the others to join us before I replay it," Kevin told me. He sounded despondent, and I got the feeling it pained him to tell me whatever he'd learned.

As if on cue, the door opened and in walked Franco, Lucas, Ivan, and Jonesy. Kevin hit play and turned up the volume.

Police have confirmed a body found by dog walkers in marshland near Fellbrook Woods in Doncaster is believed to be that of missing teen, Sarah Crowther. Fifteen-year-old Sarah was reported missing from a local residential children's home, The Willows, twelve weeks ago, along with another resident, seventeen-year-old Tess Robertson. Police at the scene were unavailable for comment, but early reports suggest that the teenager may have been murdered.

Kevin stopped the video there and proceeded to show me a new missing person appeal for Tess. It stated they believed she was in danger and wanted people to come forward if they had any information about her or her whereabouts, however insignificant they thought that might be.

Fuck, this was it! The carefully constructed bubble I'd built around Tess since she'd saved my life had burst. I shook my head, speech evading me for a moment.

"Boss, we're gonna need to get the recording and letter

from Farid Ali to the police as soon as possible. No one knows she's here, so we'll have a few days to think about how we protect her going forward," Franco said with a sigh.

Jonesy shook his head. "Not being funny, Franco, but it only takes one of the nurses at the hospital to see this news report and the photo of Tess. She's hardly someone who blends into the background with all that red hair and those pretty eyes. She had us guarding her the whole time, and the boss was there night and day. It won't take long before they come looking for her here or at the hotel. They'll either think Tess has met the same fate as that other poor girl or she's involved in her death somehow. Either way, the police won't fail to act if they get reports that she went home with the boss."

Jonesy was correct: the police had no choice but to act, and quickly. We couldn't be complacent about this, not anymore.

"Lucas, I need you to take the letter and recording to the police force who are dealing with the investigation. Obviously, we need to deliver it anonymously, but I want it done tonight in case Tariq and Hassan Akbar try to make a run for it."

"Okay, boss, I'm on it. It'll take about three hours by car, give or take. There's the foster mother, too. Has anyone contacted her to see if the police have been in touch? She might be able to tell us if the boys in blue have had anything to say about Tess."

"I called her about ten minutes ago on the burner phone you gave her, but either she didn't have it on her, or she was with the police and couldn't talk. I can try her again now," Kevin said, tapping the keyboard and putting the call on speakerphone.

"Hello?" Jean answered in a tearful voice.

"Hello, Jean, it's Kolya. I assume from the sound of your voice you have received news of the body the police have found. I am so sorry for your loss."

I heard Jean choke back a sob before trying to clear her throat.

"The police have just left. They were here almost an hour this time, asking me the same questions over and over. I have to go to the station later and make another statement about when I last saw the girls. I already did that when they first went missing. I don't know why they'd think I'd change my statement now. If they'd actually investigated when Tess told the authorities about Sarah and those men, then she'd still be alive."

Jean started crying again, so I let her have a few moments, saddened beyond belief that this poor, caring woman was alone in her grief. I glanced at Lucas, an idea forming that would benefit all concerned.

"Jean, my team and I have been collecting evidence against these men. I'm sending one of my guards, Lucas, to deliver it to the station. He needs to do so anonymously, so it doesn't implicate us. We are linked to Tess, so if it was found to have come from us, it could cast her in an unfavourable light as far as the investigation goes. If Lucas can accompany you to the station, he could find a way to leave it unseen. If we post the evidence, we risk losing it, and the delay would allow these men to go into hiding."

"Yes, of course. It needs to be delivered straight to them. He could pick me up and escort me inside the station. I could make some comment about him being a good neighbour for dropping me off or something. To be honest, those on the front desk seem quite ignorant. Like they hate doing that job and can't be bothered to make the effort. Or because they've seen so many drunken fools and can't wait for their shift to be over. It might take them a while to notice if someone had left something."

"Perfect. I will make sure Lucas has your number and address. He should be there in around three hours. I would feel better if you had someone with you tonight. He cannot stay at your home in case the police come back, but I am happy to book a suite in a nearby hotel for you both."

"I don't want to be a burden, Kolya; I know you're a very busy man. I'm glad you have Tess with you. I know I can't say anything to the police about her whereabouts, but knowing she's safe means everything to me. I have a place in my heart for all the children I've fostered over the years. But Sarah and Tess..."

Jean started crying again, but I didn't have time to give her words of comfort.

I made my apologies and once again expressed my sorrow over her loss, then made my way to the study to retrieve the package for Lucas. I wanted this done as quickly as possible, so he needed to leave immediately.

No sooner had I handed the package over to Lucas than I

heard Tess call out my name. She knocked, then opened the door slowly, as if expecting to find something she didn't want to see. It was as if she knew, somehow, because when her eyes met mine, I could already see the pain behind them.

"Kolya, what's going on? It's Sarah, isn't it? Or is it Jean? Has she had another heart attack? Please, Kolya, tell me what's wrong. I asked Jonesy and Franco, but they told me I needed to speak to you. That's when I knew it had something to do with me and not your business."

My brave Tess. She held her head high and looked deep into my eyes as she asked me those questions. Only the quiver in her whisper-soft tone gave away her fear of the answer.

James came striding into my office, quickly followed by Brad.

"What's going on, Dad? Everyone's walking around like someone stole their winning lottery ticket."

"James, I need to speak with Tess before I explain everything. She needs to hear it first."

"But…"

I interrupted him before he could question me any further.

"James, go to the tech room and tell Kevin to let you know what's going on. I need to speak to Tess on her own. I'm sorry, son, but once you find out why, you will understand."

He nodded his head, then turned to leave, pausing at the door before coming back into the room, enveloping Tess in a tight hug.

"Whatever it is, Tess, you know I'll be there for you if you need me," he told her.

Brad shot me a glance as he hovered in the doorway. I

knew he wanted to come in and offer Tess some comfort, but he was smart enough to leave it for now. My earlier display of possessiveness had the desired effect, it seemed.

I waited until Brad and James closed the door behind them before guiding Tess to the small, comfortable sofa, and taking a seat beside her.

I took her shaking hands in mine and kissed her fingertips.

"Tess, there is no easy way to say this, but earlier today, Sarah's body was discovered in marshland near Doncaster."

Tess closed her eyes without saying a word. She remained that way for thirty seconds or so, the only giveaway of her feelings being the lone tear sliding down her cheek.

"How did she die?" she asked, still not opening her eyes. As if keeping them closed made her able to cope with her obvious grief.

I sighed, closing my own eyes. Hoping that mirroring her actions would help me cope too.

It didn't.

I was unsure how much I should tell her right now. Would it be wiser to wait until she had the chance to process the loss of her friend? Or should I tell her everything—including the fact I'd learned of Sarah's death from Farid Ali before ordering his own death and disposing of his body?

Would she fear me? Hate me? Or would she accept I was only trying to keep her safe, giving her enough time to recover from her injury before she had to face the world again?

I decided on the truth.

The whole truth!

She *needed* to know the depths of depravity these men had sunk to and the threat they had posed to her safety. I had to show her a copy of the letter. She also needed to know I'd killed the man who signed it. And I would kill for her again, should the need arise.

26

TESS

I barely made it to the bathroom, throwing up until there was nothing left but bile. Kolya knelt beside me, holding back my hair, whispering soothing words while gently rubbing my back.

How is it possible that someone so caring—someone I'd trusted—could order a person's death and keep the knowledge of my best friend's murder from me? What kind of man did that make him?

I'd built him up on a pedestal and made him like a superhero.

I was naïve. Foolish. Gullible. My inexperience revealed how incredibly trusting I'd been to become so reliant on a virtual stranger all those weeks ago.

Kolya left my side for a moment and brought me a glass of water, encouraging me to drink. I did so reluctantly, not sure whether any act of kindness from him was welcome right now.

"I'd like to be alone for a while," I told him. Refusing to meet his concerned gaze.

"Tess, I need you to speak to me. To let me know how you feel about all you've just heard and seen."

"I can't do that, Kolya, because I don't even know myself how I feel right now," I told him, taking another sip of water and praying it would stay down.

"I need to know you understand why I did what I did."

"Kolya, you kept my foster sister's death from me. Her body was left to rot out in the open for months. No one had the chance to mourn her because no one who fucking cared about her knew!" I was breathing heavily, my hand gripping the glass so hard I thought it would break.

"I told you why I couldn't let anyone know. You needed time to recover, to get over your injury. I couldn't risk you being taken in for questioning while you were hurting. You know they won't let you come back here if they take you in. You'll have to go back to The Willows or some other place. I need you here so I can protect you. Your safety and well-being have been my priority since the first time I held you in my arms, your blood soaking through my clothes. When I learned about the men who'd followed you to London, and why they had done so, I was determined I'd rid you of the threat they posed. But when I heard what that despicable man and his friends had planned for you—what they had done to your friend and others—I could not let him live to carry out that threat."

"So, you became judge, jury, and executioner! How do you sleep at night knowing you ended a man's life?"

"Better than I would if he still walked the earth!"

I shook my head. This was getting us nowhere.

"I don't understand how you could keep Sarah's death from me. Didn't you trust me enough with the truth?"

"I trust you with my life, Tess. But as you've said, the fact that Sarah's body has lain undiscovered for so long has hurt you. You would have wanted to report it if you knew, which is only to be expected. She was your dear friend and foster sister, so I can understand your anger. But we had to consider all our options, and we needed to know you were safe. I am sorry you are hurting, and in a way, I do regret keeping it from you. But I was willing to risk your anger and hate to know you were safe. Sarah was already gone. There was nothing we could do for her except protect her best friend. From what you have told me about your last conversation with her, that was something she tried to do herself."

Kolya paused for a moment, rubbing his hand over his face. "I made sure that Jean and Danny—people who'd shown you love and friendship and who cared for you when no one else could—were well taken care of. I didn't want their welfare to be a cause of worry and stress for you. They are both good people who did not deserve the wrath of the ogres who were looking for you. Too many living souls could have suffered if this wasn't timed just right. You more than any.

"I was going to send the information to the police two weeks ago. But then James announced he'd be coming home for his birthday, and I didn't want the chaos that would surround these revelations to be going on while he was here. You are both so important to me; the reason my heart still beats. I did not want your first meeting to be overshadowed by grief and police interviews. But now it seems that is out of my hands, and for that, too, I am sorry."

"I… I just don't know what to say about all this. It feels like a betrayal. Like everything I thought to be true is a lie," I told him.

Those ice-blue eyes bore into mine; his hand coming up to cup my cheek. I flinched slightly, so he paused, his palm only an inch away from my skin.

"Just answer me this, Tess. Despite what you're feeling right now about all I have told you, do you believe I had only your best interests at heart?"

"I honestly don't know, Kolya. You've controlled every aspect of my life since I got shot. So much of that I'll be eternally grateful for. But keeping all this from me is just too big. You shouldn't have had the power to do what you did. You shouldn't have the power you have over me."

"Out of every sentence spoken today, that is the greatest untruth of all. My darling Tess, it is you who holds all the power here. You have done since the day we met, despite the trauma and pain surrounding it."

He leaned back against the tiled wall of the bathroom, staring at his hands. "I have long since stopped trying to work out why that is so. Why I feel that you—or thoughts of you—control so many of my actions, when clearly, I should be old enough, if not wise enough, to know better."

I swallowed hard. His words were melting into the icy wall I'd hidden my heart behind. Should I believe him? After all, he'd kept devastating yet important information from me because he believed it was in my *best interests*. Would he do so again in the future?

"I don't know if I can trust what you say anymore, Kolya. I let my guard down with you when I should have known better. I appreciate that you thought you were doing the right thing by withholding the information, but it was my life you were manipulating. I couldn't ask for better care than I've received since being here. You've made me feel like I belong, and for someone who has no family, I will be eternally grateful for that."

"You *do* have a family now. You have me and James, Nan and Jack. My entire staff adore you. A family doesn't have to be something you are born into or create. It can be something that develops over time."

"Will I have to go back to The Willows?" I asked, bracing myself for his answer.

"No!" he replied vehemently. "I will not allow it. Do you hear me, Tess?" he cried as he darted towards me. He crushed me to his chest, the glass of water I held tumbling to the floor from the sudden, unexpected movement.

"But if the police come for me, I won't have a choice, will I? I could run away again," I suggested. "That way, you can stay out of it. You could tell them you came home one day and I'd left."

It wasn't something I wanted to think about, but I knew I might not have a choice once the police arrived. Going back to The Willows wasn't an option for me. Brad said I had choices. Well, I choose not to go back into care. Whatever I had to do to keep out of the grasp of social services, I would.

"I will not let them take you, Tess. I will do anything to keep you here. Anything at all. For God's sake, I killed a man to keep you safe, and I would do so again, without hesitation. I'd give the whole world to keep you with me."

"Kolya," I sobbed. The depth of emotion in his words gave me hope for something I had only ever dreamed of, never expecting I would get to experience it.

Utter devotion! Whether it came from the fact I'd saved his life or something else entirely.

I had to forgive Kolya and let him do everything he could to keep me here. Despite my earlier thoughts and protestations, a battle with the authorities was something I couldn't win on my own. But with Kolya by my side, although saddened beyond belief, I felt anything was possible.

27

KOLYA

My solicitor, Oliver Ward-Jones, sat patiently taking notes in my study while Tess retold the story of why she left the children's home and ran away to London. He'd arrived barely an hour after I'd finished breaking the news of Sarah's death to her. Tess was heartbroken. But the fact I'd known Sarah was dead so many weeks ago was something she found hard to come to terms with. Oddly enough, that seemed to bother her more than the reason Farid Ali was dead.

Tess is an enigma. Just when I think I know her, she surprises me once again.

It was Nan's day off today, but as soon as she found out what happened, she came over from her cottage on the estate to comfort Tess.

I'd given them some time alone while I'd taken Oliver into my study. I wanted to fill him in on everything we'd learned so far. When Oliver was ready to see Tess, I came out to find her sitting on the sofa with Nan and Ivan—his big arms wrapped around them both as they cried together. Danny and Bess sat by their feet, leaning back against them.

Jonesy caught me in the doorway before I entered.

"It was hard enough to hear her and Nan cry, boss, but when Ivan started sniffling, I was out of there. I couldn't cope if he cried. I'd sooner face insurgents than be around to see that."

Jonesy left me standing there, staring at the outpouring of both grief and love, grateful to see that Tess had so many people in her life who genuinely cared. Something she'd been missing for so long.

I interrupted their touching moment to bring Tess into my study to see Oliver. I was introduced to him by my late wife; they had been friends since childhood. Oliver's father—also a solicitor—had handled all the legal work for the Lassiter Hotel Group, so it made perfect sense that I use them for KOLCAT Engineering.

Oliver was at the top of his game with all the legal work needed in my business, so I wasn't sure if he would bring someone else in to advise us on how to proceed with our current situation. I'd already spoken to him about Tess, telling him about her ordeal and about what I had learned from Farid Ali, although he understood that wasn't on the record, and I hadn't informed him of the man's death.

I worried that Oliver's methods and manner would be a little too aggressive for Tess while she was still so upset, but as the minutes ticked by, my concern abated.

He listened carefully, recording the conversation and

taking notes, and when asking Tess to clarify something, he did so in a mild, apologetic manner. Most unlike the Oliver I dealt with professionally. Perhaps being the father of a teenage daughter helped when having to interview young women.

That's how Tess looked to me at this very moment: young and vulnerable. Not only did my heart ache for her and what she had gone through, but I also felt bad for my actions earlier. I would have kissed her in the pool if we'd not been interrupted. I'd wanted to press my body against hers to let her feel what effect just the thought of her had on me every day. But relaying the information about her friend and what she went through made me feel sick.

For a moment or two, I compared myself to those men. After all, I'd been lusting after a girl who wasn't old enough to vote. I'd always given her my full attention, showered her with gifts, and bestowed upon her enough love and affection to last a lifetime. Isn't that what men who groom young girls do?

Before today I'd never let my desire for her show. I knew the age of consent in the UK was sixteen, yet to me, they're still a child at that age. Tess will be eighteen in a matter of months. An adult. But she's not there yet.

Jealousy had taken over me earlier. I'd been jealous of a young man more suited to her age group. A young man who did not deserve to be on the receiving end of the anger I felt. But I knew I would feel the same if I saw anyone else flirting with her.

Tess is mine! It is as simple as that. Nothing more needs to happen to convince me of it. However, I knew I should do the honourable thing and keep away from her in *that* way until her eighteenth. I would feel more comfortable expressing my desire for her after she reaches that milestone. I can only fool myself so much and say her life experiences have made her more mature in mind than someone of her age should be. Though some can argue the truth of that, there would be others who would say she'd need to experience how it feels to be a carefree teen before she can embrace what it means to be a woman.

Oliver went over a few of the notes he'd made with Tess, and while he did so, I came to a decision. I would be strong, for her sake if nothing else. I would keep my growing sexual need for her hidden until she was ready for me, however long that might take.

I was still deep in thought when I heard Oliver call out my name.

"Kolya, as I've just told Tess, it's likely that her face and details will be all over the national news by morning, if not by the late bulletin tonight. So it's best if she goes to the station dealing with the case as soon as possible."

"But if I do that, I won't be able to come back here until I'm eighteen," Tess cried, the fear she tried so bravely to hide becoming clear.

Franco stepped forward and squeezed her shoulder in reassurance, though his clenched jaw showed his unease with the situation.

"No, Oliver, I will not allow it. There has to be some other way." We'd gone over this several times since Tess came to stay, and each time, his answer did not differ from the last.

"Kolya, neither you nor your staff are approved foster carers. To become so often takes months, sometimes years. And I doubt very much that someone who creates and sells weapons would be considered suitable."

"What about Tess's grandmother? Doesn't she have legal rights?" I asked. "I would be happy to approach the woman and offer her money to sign guardianship over to me if possible."

"Kolya, again, if it *was* possible, which it most certainly is not, given the fact her grandmother is in prison, and the state has legal responsibility over Tess, it would still take time we don't have."

Oliver sighed, reaching over to take Tess's hand in his. "Tess, I wish there was something we could do within the law to keep you here. We could say you fear for your life, given the circumstances, and that Kolya will provide you with safe refuge. But it's unlikely they will let you return. The only way to overturn any legal responsibility the state or family members have over you is if you were to marry. If that were to happen, your husband would become legally responsible for your care, as you, in turn, would be responsible for his."

"But I'm too young to get married, and I don't even have a boyfriend, so that won't happen."

Tess sat back in her chair, her shoulders sagging.

"You can get married at sixteen, but in England, you need parental consent. In Scotland, you wouldn't need it," Oliver stated. His brow furrowed as he seemed to consider something. I saw him glance across at Franco, who stood watching them quietly.

"I'll marry you, Tess," Franco offered resolutely.

"No! If anyone's going to be marrying Tess, it's me," I told him, then I glanced at Tess to determine her reaction.

"Kolya, as your solicitor, I must advise against it," Oliver quickly interjected, looking a little flustered.

"Hang on, everyone. This is my life you're all discussing here. Don't I get a say in it?" Tess questioned.

I walked over to where she sat and knelt before her. Taking her hands in mine, I looked into her tear-filled eyes.

"Tess, I know this isn't something you'd have wished for —getting married as a legal necessity—but I won't risk you being taken from me. Or from here, a place where you sleep safely at night. In no time at all, you'll be eighteen and will answer to no one. When that time comes, you can abandon the marriage if that's what you want."

I watched as she swallowed nervously. Her eyes darted first to Oliver, then to Franco. "Kolya, I know I saved your life, but you've done enough to repay me already. I can't let you do this. It's too much."

"Tess, I want to do this. I could not rest knowing you were out there without me or my guards. None of us could. Nan would be inconsolable, and we wouldn't want to cause Danny any more stress and worry—not when he's doing so well. Please, Tess, agree to become my wife. For however long you want or need the name Mrs Tess Barinov."

Everyone waited with bated breath until Tess nodded slowly. Oliver cleared his throat before advising me on legal issues. He had his laptop open and was currently looking through what we would need to do to marry in Scotland.

"You have to submit a request to marry to the Registrar General at least twenty-nine days before the date you want to marry. Although it does state that in exceptional circumstances, the Registrar General can authorise a marriage to take place without the twenty-nine days' notice."

Oliver carried on tapping at his keyboard for a few seconds, then paused, looking up at me with a grin. "Guess who the District Registrar for Glengarran is? It's Thomas Murray!"

I thought back to a conversation I had with Thomas—the local mayor—when I first became the owner of Glengarran Castle. He was a man who wasn't too proud to ask for monetary assistance to keep the village and nearby town thriving. As money was not an issue for me, I agreed to fund the cost of repairs to the local school, as well as a new parish room for the priest, Father Creahan.

I meet with both men socially on my visits to Glengarran. They also have permission to fish the loch and use the golf course on my estate whenever they like. I could almost guarantee they'd bend the rules in order to keep that permission—and my regular donations to the church and council.

"I will call Thomas and Father Creahan now," I announced. "Oliver, gather any legal documents we'll need to present so the marriage can take place. Getting a birth certificate for Tess is a priority. Once we have that, there should be no issue."

"Jean has a copy of my birth certificate," Tess informed us. "She got a spare when I stayed with her so I could use it to get my school bus pass and a card for the library."

"Excellent. Lucas can collect it from her before he leaves. Now, please excuse me while I speak with Thomas and Father Creahan. Although I believe that money will do more of the talking in those conversations. We need to get the whole thing organised as soon as possible. Oliver, I know it's getting late, but I need you to source the necessary paperwork."

I turned to Tess and smiled.

"My darling, you'll need to find a wedding dress. There's a dress shop in the village about four miles from here. Nan is a friend of the owner and often does the alterations on some of the wedding and prom dresses. I'm sure you've seen the photographs she has on her phone of those she's worked on. She does delight in showing everyone her work. Perhaps the owner would open up the shop for you tonight or early in the morning? Nan can arrange it."

"Kolya, I… Are you sure about this?" Tess asked. She was looking at me as if I was some sort of conundrum she was trying to figure out. As if she knew there was another reason I'd marry so quickly, other than the danger she was in. My wife-to-be is an intelligent woman, of that there is no doubt. I *do* have an ulterior motive.

I want her to be mine in more than just my thoughts and dreams. I will rest much easier when the entire world knows she belongs to me.

Once we are married, I'll take her to my favourite restaurants, show her off to all my family and friends, and introduce her as my wife—someone who promised to forsake all others as long as we both shall live. And in a house of God, no less.

If I get my way, and I nearly always do, we will fly to

Scotland tomorrow and marry in the church at Glengarran. Then Tess and I can begin the rest of our lives as husband and wife.

Tess left the room with Franco, promising to reveal all to Nan so they could begin their search for a dress. She still seemed a little bewildered, but as Tess once told me herself, she is one of life's copers. I had no doubt she would cope with her grief and this new development in her usual stoic manner.

"Kolya, if you *are* going ahead with all this, we need to talk about a prenuptial agreement. Currently, they're not legally binding in England, but a judge will try to uphold one where they see fit."

"I don't need a prenup, Oliver. Tess is not out to take me for everything I have."

"I'm sorry, Kolya, but as your solicitor, I need to caution you against not having any sort of written agreement in place for when you divorce."

"Tess and I won't be getting a divorce. Not when she's eighteen and can live her own life; not ever, in fact."

"Is Tess aware of this? Because it seemed as though she and everyone here understood this will be a marriage of convenience."

Oliver stared at me for a moment, waiting for an answer. I did not give one. He ran his hands through his hair before tilting his head back with a sigh.

"You're in love with her, aren't you?"

"Yes."

"Jesus, Kolya, she's young enough to be your daughter. Younger than your son. How will James feel about all this? He'll have a stepmother who is two years younger than him."

"James will accept it. He likes Tess."

"As a friend, maybe. But this is something else entirely. And for his sake, I insist you let me draw up a prenup."

"Okay. Tess can have Glengarran and a million a year until she remarries. How does that sound?"

"Are you taking this fucking seriously, Kolya?"

"Deadly. If we ever divorce, I wouldn't want to be somewhere that reminds me of our wedding. And it would be worth more than a million a year to see her remain single."

"Why, Kolya? Why have you fallen so hard for her? You've only known her for three months. Is it because she saved your life? Do you feel guilty that she was hurt by a bullet meant for you?"

"Yes, of course I have guilt over Tess being shot, but that's not the reason I feel so strongly about her. I can't really explain it. I felt a connection with her the first time I looked into her eyes as she lay bleeding before me. Since that first night in the hospital when I sat beside her, our connection has grown.

"Tess and I have something special: a bond that cannot be broken, no matter what happens in the future. I'm not asking you to understand it; neither am I asking you to condone it. But despite whatever you or anyone else thinks, I am determined to make Tess my wife."

28

TESS

The church at Glengarran was small and quaint. I was grateful for that. If it had been large and imposing, I think my nerves would have got the better of me. As it was, I found myself shaking as I heard Father Creahan ask Kolya to repeat vows that would have meant so much to me if this marriage were real. Well, perhaps real wasn't the right word to use. It most certainly was real. In the legal sense, anyway.

"...take Tess Robertson as your lawfully wedded wife. To have and to hold from this day forward, for better, for worse, for richer, for poorer, in sickness and in health, to love and to cherish, until death do you part?"

"I do!" Kolya's answer was loud and clear, leaving the priest and everyone in the limited pews no room for doubt.

But now it was my turn. From the expectant look on Father Creahan's face, I could tell he was confident he'd receive the same answer. My mouth was dry, and despite the coolness of the church, I was a little too warm.

Even though I'd been standing in one place for so long, my heart was beating fast. It felt as though I'd been running, the pounding of my pulse like a rapid drumbeat. I looked to my right and saw Nan and Jack—both smiling, although they seemed slightly confused. Turning to my left, I saw the priest, also confused. For a moment I wondered why, then I realised he'd stopped speaking.

"I do!" I half whispered, my voice croaky. There was a collective sigh of relief from everyone in the church. Everyone but me, that is.

I looked up to find Kolya smiling, but it didn't quite reach his beautiful blue eyes. Perhaps he'd thought I might not say I do? I smiled back at him, trying to reassure him I wasn't about to run for the hills.

There was enough of them around the place. Hills, I mean. As well as fields, forests, and lochs. Inverness had the prettiest scenery I'd ever seen, and Glengarran Castle was the icing on the cake. If I were Kolya, I'd live there all the time. It was stunning. So much more so than it looked on the security monitors.

The front and side of the castle had the same dark-grey weathered stone as the church, and I'd seen the same coloured stone in the shops and cottages in Glengarran village. I couldn't wait to go back and explore. We didn't have time earlier, and there won't be time tomorrow once I've contacted the police.

We'd flown by helicopter to Glossop, Derbyshire, to meet

Jean, before continuing our journey to Glengarran. We spent a tearful, hug-filled hour together—something I think Jean and I needed.

Sadly, Jean couldn't come here with us. Kolya said if the police found out she'd been at our wedding, they would suspect she'd known of my whereabouts all along. I didn't want her charged with withholding information, so I had to be content with the short time I spent with her on my *special day*.

Lucas had been staying in a hotel with Jean for the past two nights, as Kolya had been worried about repercussions from the information the police had received.

There had been nothing on the news about it until this afternoon—two days after they'd received the damning statement. Hassan was arrested a few hours ago in connection to Sarah's death.

The police had also appealed for any information regarding the whereabouts of Tariq and Farid. They, too, were *wanted in connection* to Sarah's death, but I knew they could only ever catch and punish one of them.

The very person responsible for Farid's death had been praying to God just a few minutes ago, having insisted we get married in a church. Obviously, Kolya must believe God overlooks such things as murder. Maybe he thought the ten commandments were just suggestions, not rules?

I'd decided not to ask too many questions about it. There was nothing that could be done, anyway, and the more Kolya said the man deserved to die, the more I believed it. What I had a hard time coming to terms with was how someone as sweet and loving as Kolya could take a life. As if it was his right. Was there something about him I just wasn't seeing? Something that was glaringly obvious to someone else, but not to me?

The wedding ring Kolya placed on my finger caught the light from the stained-glass window and sparkled prettily. The band was rose gold, set with a channel of diamonds, giving it enough bling without it being too ostentatious.

The one I placed on Kolya's finger was in brushed rose gold with a platinum channel. It looked good on him. He already had a ring he wore on the third finger of his right hand: a white gold signet ring set with a Cyrillic B for Barinov. My surname now, too, I thought, as the priest pronounced us husband and wife.

"You may kiss your bride," proclaimed Father Creahan, as if it meant nothing. To me, that couldn't be further from the truth.

Kolya took me in his arms, pulling me flush against his body.

"Mrs Barinov," he said with a smile, then kissed me full on the mouth. I expected a peck on the lips, maybe one that lingered a little. Instead, with his hand at the back of my neck, he held me close, pressing his soft, full lips against mine in a way that caused my mouth to open, allowing his tongue to brush over mine, once, twice, three times, until I felt myself almost melt into him. My lips held no resistance when he took the kiss further, and despite it being the first time I'd done this, I was surprised by how right it felt… and how easy it was to kiss him back.

I heard Father Creahan cough behind us, which was our

cue to separate. Not that I wanted to. I'd have willingly carried on kissing him despite the audience if it felt like that every time.

Breathing heavily and with a shaking hand, I placed my fingertips over my lips. They felt so much fuller. Sensitive. Perfectly right.

I looked up to find Kolya watching me closely, his eyes following the path of my fingers as they traced my lips. The way he looked at me… It was different. Intense.

"Kolya?" I questioned, my voice breaking with emotion. I wanted to know what this meant for us and why he'd kissed me so passionately.

I watched as his expression changed, becoming serious. Then he gave me a smile I knew to be fake before whispering in my ear, "We have to put on a show, Tess. They need to believe it's real!"

Just like that, my heart sank, and despite the room full of people, I'd never felt more alone in my life.

29

TESS

The housekeeper at Glengarran, Mrs Braeburn, didn't like me. Oh, she was polite, especially in front of Kolya, but she was standoffish every other time. Like she looked at me and found me lacking.

I couldn't care less, to be honest.

She didn't seem to like Nan either, which said more for Mrs Braeburn's character than it did about Nan, who nearly everyone loved.

The staff at Glengarran didn't know the reason for our wedding. Kolya said it was better that way. The fewer people who knew, the less we'd have to worry about the police finding out. Not that Kolya didn't trust his staff at Glengarran, but there are different levels of trust, some of which are born through time and circumstance. Kolya rarely spent more than six weeks a year at Glengarran, and he spent little time with the staff when he *was* in residence. He said the people there were old school, in an Upstairs Downstairs/Downton Abbey kind of way.

Their previous employer was a ninety-five-year-old laird who'd employed generations of the same families to work in both the castle and on the estate. Mrs Braeburn had been his housekeeper for thirty years, so she was loyal, if nothing else.

She turned her nose up at my dress, which wasn't a traditional white flowing gown. Well, let's be honest, my new husband might own a castle, but this was hardly a fairy-tale relationship.

I'd fallen in love with my dress as soon as I'd seen it, although the price tag put me off. At nearly three thousand pounds, I thought it was way too much to pay, but Kolya told Nan I was to have whatever I wanted. So, the vintage-looking shell-pink strapless dress, with deep-cream lace, became mine. Marion, the lady who owned the dress shop, provided me with matching heels and a lace shawl, which she attached to the edge of my dress on the left side, draping it over my shoulder, effectively covering the scar left from the bullet wound. Vintage pink underwear my husband would never get to see, along with silk stockings, completed my outfit.

Nan had given me the pearl earrings and necklace she'd worn on her wedding day, which had been my *something borrowed*. My despondent mood being the *something blue*.

Apart from the pearls, I had nothing old, although the castle surrounding me fit the bill perfectly. Just looking at it made me feel at peace. As if they'd built it here in these beautiful surroundings with me in mind.

The staff at Glengarran had done an excellent job of organising our wedding reception—given that they had only two days in which to do so.

Getting the District Registrar to agree to our wedding *without* the statutory twenty-nine days' notice would never have been a hard task for someone with Kolya's wealth. Not that Thomas Murray was a greedy man; he wanted nothing for himself. But he hinted enough to Kolya that the local pensioners' guild would benefit from a new minibus to take them to and from the market and for hospital appointments.

It was Father Creahan who presented more of a problem. He wanted proof that I was Catholic before agreeing to marry us. Lucas and Jean had to visit the priest at the church where I'd been baptised to gather the relevant information.

My grandmother—although the biggest drug dealer in our town—was also a devout Catholic who never missed church on Sundays. She insisted on me being baptised, so I suppose I had her to thank for the fact I could get married here today.

Mum used to say that religion had been my grandmother's downfall. They caught her selling cocaine to three of the altar boys, so in a way, she was right.

I've never kept in touch with my grandmother. In fact, I detest the woman and blamed her for my mother's drug addiction. I'd often seen her slip Mum the odd wrap or two, even after she'd come out of rehab, knowing that once Mum had taken whatever she'd given her, I'd be left to look after myself.

What kind of grandparent does that?

As far as I'm concerned, the woman is poison. She's the kind of person who family and society are better off without.

The air here in Inverness was so much fresher than in Oxford. We'd had dinner in the castle's large, oak-panelled dining room, then came out into the garden for drinks and dancing.

The gamekeeper's father had played the bagpipes on our return from church, which Kolya was thrilled about. I had to admit it was a nice touch, and definitely something to remember. The piper's name was John, and he told me so many tales of his life here on the estate, both as a boy helping his father on the shoots, and then when he, himself, had been the gamekeeper. The job had certainly been a tradition in their family, and one which John was extremely proud of. I liked him. He was genuine. As was his son—also called John. Both were now well on their way to being drunk, and their accents grew so much stronger as the drinks flowed.

I left the party and made my way down to the loch, wondering how long it would take one of Kolya's guards to join me. As it turns out, it was about thirty seconds.

"How come you left the party?" Franco asked before launching a small stone that skimmed the surface of the loch.

"Had enough," I admitted, then nodded back towards the guests. "Go back and have a few drinks. You don't need to babysit me."

"Nah, I'm good. I can't tell what the fuck those Scottish guys are saying, anyway."

I laughed, teasing him about his own accent. Franco was

the epitome of every Italian American gangster movie I'd ever seen. With his black hair, brown eyes and heavy New Jersey accent, he could have walked straight off a mafia movie set. When he got annoyed or frustrated with me, his accent became even stronger. I'd often mimic him, which made him laugh.

Franco smiling and laughing is something every woman should see. The man is gorgeous, and he knows it.

All the guards had worn suits today—something Kolya should have them do all the time, not just when they accompany him on business. They were definitely worth a second look, with Franco being the hottest of them all.

"So, Tess, how do you feel about today? The wedding, I mean?"

I shrugged my shoulders because, truth be told, I didn't really know how to feel about my fake wedding that wasn't really fake.

"Do you regret it?" he asked.

"It wasn't what I wanted," I told him truthfully.

"You could have married me. I did offer," he said in all seriousness.

I held his gaze, waiting for some smart remark I was sure would follow. It didn't.

"You were serious about that?" I questioned.

"Wouldn't have offered if I wasn't."

"But why, Franco? Why would you offer to marry someone you don't even love?"

He looked away for a moment before he answered, skimming another stone across the water.

"I did it because you needed me, and I wanted to do it."

"I don't understand. Are you yet another man who feels guilty because I got shot? Like you have something to atone for?"

"Wasn't me who agreed to let those fucking idiots do lead detail that day! I got nothing to atone for, sweetheart."

"I don't know how that would have worked, us being married. I don't even know how this will work. With Kolya, I mean," I told him.

"Sure you do, Tess. We all saw this coming. It was gonna happen with or without the threats to you."

"What do you mean?" I asked, confused.

"Honey, I don't know how innocent you are, but you must know that when a man looks at you the way the boss does, he wants to be doing a whole lot more than holding your hand," Franco said with a smirk.

"You're wrong," I told him.

"How about that kiss in church? I'd say a man who kisses his bride like that is planning on being inside her on their wedding night."

"All for show, Franco." I was taken aback by how forward he was being. It wasn't like him at all.

"Is that what he said? That it was for show? Then he was lying to you or himself. Probably both. Sweetheart, for you, the boss is all in. Question is, what do *you* want? If this isn't it, you sign whatever papers are needed and get the hell away as soon as you turn eighteen."

"What if I want to stay?"

"Then you better make sure you're staying for the right reasons."

"I'd miss you all if I left. This is the only family I have, apart from Jean. I don't know if I could give you all up." It hurt to even think about it. But if Kolya wanted a divorce when I turned eighteen, I might not have a choice.

Franco took my hand. "You ain't getting rid of me that easy. Besides, you can't shoot for shit, so I need to keep up your lessons."

"That is *so* not true," I stated, laughing as I bent at the knees, scooping up water from the loch and splashing him.

"What the fuck, Tess? I swear if you weren't wearing such a pretty dress, I'd pick you up and throw you in." Franco was grinning wickedly, and I could tell he was tempted to do just that. But I loved this dress, and I didn't think a dip in the loch would do it any good.

"Hey, guys, what are you doing down here? You're missing the party," Brad yelled, walking swiftly towards us.

"Oh, fuck! That's all you need," Franco muttered under his breath.

"What do you mean?" I whispered.

"Come on, Tess. You must have noticed that the boss hates Brad being near you when he's not around."

I shrugged my shoulders as Brad approached. I hadn't noticed anything much over the last two days. I'd been too busy.

Franco leaned in to whisper in my ear before leaving us. "I'm guessing thirty seconds, sixty tops before the boss is down here staking his claim."

He winked, then walked away, heading along the side of the loch.

"I was hoping I could dance with the bride, but when I turned around, you weren't there," Brad said.

"I wanted to get away for a few minutes. Catch my breath and all that."

Brad nodded and stared out over the water.

"Kolya seems happy, but then how could he not be? He has a beautiful new bride."

"You have a silver tongue, Brad. Do you use it on every female you meet?" I questioned, then blushed furiously when I realised the double meaning behind my words.

Brad smirked and was just about to say something when Kolya cut him off.

"James was asking where you'd gone, Brad. He told me to tell you he thinks the ghillie's daughter is a sure thing."

"Of course she is—being as I have a silver tongue and all. In fact, I think it's time I showed her what my silver tongue can do." Before he left, Brad blew me a kiss, which seemed to infuriate Kolya.

"How's James?" I asked, trying to drag his attention away from Brad's retreating form.

"He's trying to charm the cook's niece. I think her name is Dianna. He was asking her to dance with him, but she was playing hard to get."

James hadn't been happy about us getting married. From my room, I'd heard him go on a rant about my age and the reason we were doing it. He'd said if Kolya wanted to, he could find a way to hide me from the police. Kolya had disagreed with him, explaining that if I didn't come forward, they could consider me a suspect in Sarah's murder.

James said he'd always hoped if his dad ever got married again, it would be because he'd fallen in love with someone he wanted to spend the rest of his life with. That's when their voices went quiet, and I didn't hear anything else. James seemed fine about it today. He'd stood beside Kolya as his best man, which was as it should be.

I'd asked Jack to give me away. He said he'd be proud to do so, and Nan cried happy tears when he walked me down the aisle.

"You are away in your thoughts again, Tess. Tell me, my darling, what are you thinking about that keeps taking your attention away from our day?"

"Actually, I'm thinking about the wedding."

"Ahh, it was a beautiful ceremony. Wouldn't you agree?"

"Some of it," I muttered. Then added, "You and James looked so alike when I saw you at the altar. I like you in this colour; it suits you. It makes your eyes seem even bluer."

Both he and James had worn matching grey suits with ties that complemented the colour of my dress. Nan had done well in picking them out. The flowers she'd ordered had also been perfect, especially the bouquet. Pink and cream carnations with white baby's breath, surrounded by various bits of greenery and tied with deep-cream lace. Beautiful. Nan said everyone would expect me to toss the bouquet, but I didn't know if I could bring myself to do it.

"You are deep in thought again, my love. If something is bothering you, let me know so I can share your burden. After all, we are husband and wife now. It is my duty to take care of any worries or fears you have."

"Don't, Kolya."

"Don't what, my love?"

"Don't make out that what we did today matters. The vows we took, the words we repeated. We had to *'put on a show. They need to believe it's real.'* Isn't that what you said?"

I turned to walk away from him. I'd had enough. Literally.

Kolya grabbed me by the arm, yanking me back to him almost painfully.

"Do you *honestly* believe that, Tess? Did you not feel anything at all when you spoke those vows? I know what I said after I kissed you. I saw the look on your face. You were shocked. My kiss was unwelcome. I tried to make light of it to make you feel better."

"Yeah? Well, you failed. Epically!"

"I see that now, and I am truly sorry."

"This day, the big rush we had, has been so stressful. I suppose all weddings are. But with learning of Sarah's death and the worry over the police finding me… It's been too much, Kolya." I took a deep breath before admitting, "When you kissed me, which was my first proper kiss, by the way, I felt for a moment or two that everything would turn out okay and that the wedding was meant to be. But then…"

"Then I said it was all for show. I am sorry, Tess; if I could take it back, I would. But I can't, so let me make it up to you. Please?"

"How? The moment has passed. You can't do anything to change that now."

"I can kiss you again, and this time you'll know it's not for show. That it's more real than any that's ever been."

I sighed and shook my head. I'd dreamed of this a few days ago, of Kolya wanting to kiss me and so much more. But not now. Not after all this disappointment. I wanted to go to bed and forget about the day. But I also knew what tomorrow would bring when I returned to Doncaster to give my statement to the police.

"Kolya, all I want right now is for you to be my friend. I want what we had last week before all this blew up around us."

"If that's all you want, my love, then that's what I will give you. But we'll have to share a room tonight. The staff here will expect it. How about we watch a movie and chill for a while? We can grab some food on the way up. I noticed you ate very little today."

"Sounds good to me," I told him. And it did. I needed the friendship we shared, the comfort I knew I'd feel from simply having him beside me. A kiss or anything else would be too confusing right now. I needed familiarity. New and exciting experiences could wait for another day.

30

KOLYA

I hadn't planned on spending my wedding night watching vampire movies, but that's just what I had done to please my bride. *Interview with the Vampire* plus a glass of brandy and champagne had been enough to lull Tess into a deep sleep, though I wouldn't call it peaceful.

She lay next to me with her head on my chest, her coppery curls covering my upper body. Now and then, she'd tense up and whimper, which was tearing my heart in two.

What did she dream of that caused her to react so? Was it the thought of going to the police tomorrow? The death of her friend? Or had my unintended words caused her restless slumber?

In my haste to make her mine, I'd not considered that Tess would need to know of my emotional investment in our vows. I thought that baring my heart and soul would be just too much for her after everything that had happened. Not revealing my true feelings for her had tainted the whole ceremony in her eyes, and my words after I'd kissed her ruined everything else.

I did not deserve to breathe the same air as her, never mind sharing her bed. And yet, I was lying beside her on the night of our marriage, stroking her cheek as her breath fanned the hair on my chest.

My wife has a forgiving nature, although not so forgiving as to allow me to kiss her again. Not tonight, anyway.

My plan for the night had been for more of those delicious kisses while my hands roamed her body, learning the feel of the curves I'd denied myself for so long. I hadn't planned on taking it further than that. I knew Tess wasn't ready for more, and despite how much I wanted her, I could not live with myself if she ever felt pressured into sleeping with me.

Tess denied me the kisses I craved, asking me to be her friend instead. Strangely enough, that meant so much more than if she'd wanted me to make love to her all night long.

Tess needed me. She needed the comfort of our friendship, the connection that joined our very souls. We had time enough for everything else that comes with being husband and wife, and our firm, unbreakable friendship will give our marriage a solid foundation.

I know that when we finally consummate our marriage, the act will be perfection itself.

I hadn't expected Tess to be a virgin. She'd never mentioned a boyfriend, but I assumed that someone so pretty would have them queueing up to date her. Therefore, I was speechless when she told me that my kiss had been her first.

But when I thought about what that meant—that I would be the first man to touch her, to take her body with my own—I felt elated.

Before that can happen, we need to get all the upcoming police business over and done with, and then I can *take care* of those vile men who wanted to hurt my wife. Although Hassan Akbar had been arrested, I feared his brother, Tariq, had left the country. I'd placed a call through to a private investigator I knew, hoping he could shed some light on Tariq's whereabouts. If he *had* left the country, it's possible he would have fled to Pakistan.

Wherever Tariq is hiding, I will find him.

The British judicial system suffers from rules and morals I simply do not share, so I will take action, if necessary, to prevent him escaping justice—even if that means I have to serve it to him myself.

I hate to think about Tess having to make a statement tomorrow. She told me how the police had spoken to her after her mother's death—how they accused her of selling her body, believing the worst of her because of her mother's profession. She'd run from the same detectives when they came to the children's home after Sarah had gone missing. They were people who should have been protecting her instead of throwing disbelief and scorn her way.

I won't allow anyone to treat her poorly again. Tess is my queen! If I witness anyone disrespecting her, whatever rank or title they hold, I will make sure they suffer.

I will wait as patiently as I can for her while she speaks with the police, though it won't be easy. Knowing she has

Oliver going in with her will help. He will ensure she's treated fairly and with the respect she deserves. I want them to know from the start, my wife is more than just a runaway. She's a better person than they'll ever be. A decent, caring, brave young woman who means more to me than anything. The woman I love with all my heart and soul.

My wife.

My life.

My Tess.

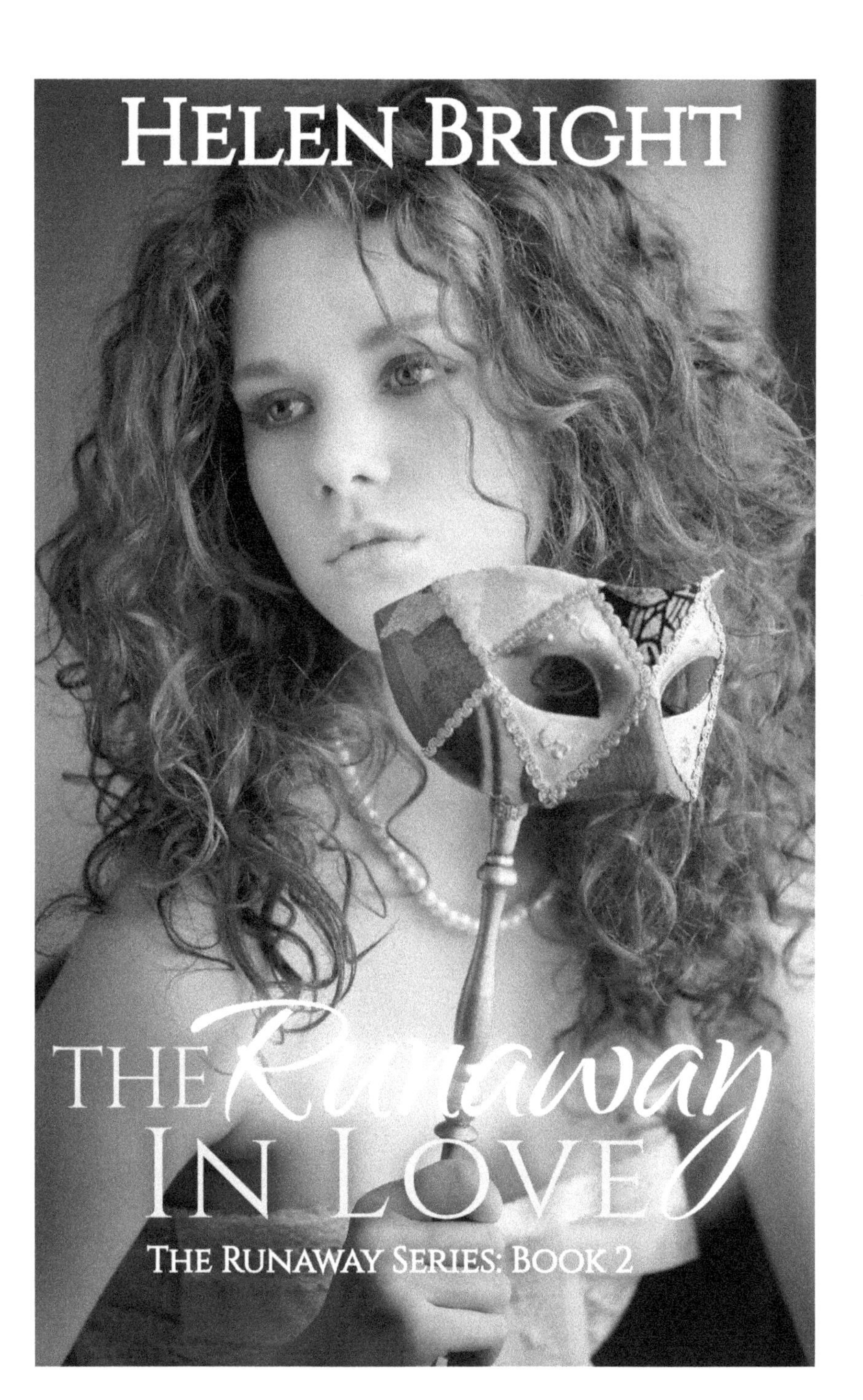
HELEN BRIGHT
THE Runaway IN LOVE
THE RUNAWAY SERIES: BOOK 2

ALSO BY HELEN BRIGHT

The Night Movers Vampire Series:

My Love Forever

Blood & Secrets

Gregor's Reason

Sergei's Angel

Cian's Journey: A Night Movers Vampire Novella

Books 5, 6, and 7 TBA

The Runaway Series

The Runaway & The Russian

The Runaway In Love

The Runaway's Ruin, Part 1

The Runaway's Ruin, Part 2

ABOUT THE AUTHOR

Helen Bright was born and raised in Yorkshire, UK, and often bases her novels in and around the county.
Whether she's writing paranormal or contemporary romance, her novels often have darker elements hidden inside a deep and meaningful love story.

For more information:

www.helenbrightauthor.co.uk

Lightning Source UK Ltd.
Milton Keynes UK
UKHW012220080123
414983UK00002B/7